Willi

MW00791136

DEFIANCE
A House Divided

Alamo Publishing

Alamo Publishing

ISBN: 978-1-926456-13-3
eISBN: 978-1-926456-12-6

Books by William H. Weber

Defiance: The Defending Home Series
Defiance: A House Divided

Last Stand: Surviving America's Collapse
Last Stand: Patriots (Book 2)
Last Stand: Warlords (Book 3)
Last Stand: Turning the Tide (Book 4)

Long Road to Survival (Book 1)
Long Road to Survival (Book 2)

Dedication

First, a heartfelt thank you to Roger Peterson, Darryl Lapidus, Tom Poulin, H. Rossi and LBC for your thoughtful comments on an early draft of the book. I'd also like to thank the ARC team once again for your dedication and your honest reviews. The final note of appreciation goes out to the fans for making all of this possible.

Book Description

Dale Hardy thought he had seen the face of evil. But that was before the virus, before the cartel. Now, with his home and family in danger, Dale must look real evil in the eyes. He must choose between sanctuary and defiance and he must unite a house divided.

Chapter 1

His hand betraying a slight tremble, Dale pushed aside the burlap curtain that covered the window and watched as the dust cloud drew nearer. No doubt, leading the charge was Edwardo Ortega. After Zach's men had been ambushed and slaughtered—save for Dannyboy and a biker who had perhaps wisely opted to flee—Ortega's objective had become as clear as the cloudless blue sky above. He and the Mexican criminals he commanded had been sent to finish what Sheriff Gaines and Mayor Reid had so unjustly started. They wanted Dale's land, but more than that, they wanted every drop of water that could be pumped from his substantial aquifer.

"How long until they're here?" Zach asked, although it sounded far more like a demand. There was a funny look in his brother-in-law's eye. It wasn't fear, though. He was yearning for revenge.

"Not nearly enough," Dale replied, moving quickly past them and down the hall to his bedroom where he collected the Remington 700 Walter had given him, along with two boxes of .30-06 rounds.

Brooke, Shane and Colton followed him, terror streaked across each of their faces.

"So what's the plan, big brother?" Shane asked, trying to sound calm and collected, but, like most things in his life, failing miserably at it.

"I'm gonna set up a shooting position from the second story of the barn," Dale told him.

"Are you insane?" his daughter Brooke said. "That's suicide." Her eyes were filling with tears.

"It's not a bad idea," Walter piped up, although the features of his weathered face wrinkled with concern. "She does have a point though. When things get hairy you may just find yourself cut off."

Dale considered this.

"Cut off," Sandy said, a hand on the grip of the 9mm pistol on her belt, "but not alone. I'm going with you."

She must've seen the rebuttal forming on his lips because she cut him off before he could get the words out. "They'll be here any moment," she said. "There isn't time to argue."

Dale gritted his teeth. "I forgot how stubborn you are." He started out of his bedroom—Duke at his heels—and paused by the top landing. "The retractable stairs aren't ready yet, so we'll head out through the garage. Colton, close and lock it after us, will you?" He turned to his daughter. "Brooke, run downstairs and grab the set of walkie-talkies from the basement."

She didn't move for a moment, until he ordered her to snap out of it and get moving.

"The rest of you," Dale said, "take your positions and conserve your ammo. We don't know how long this will last."

"Don't worry, I'll get 'em sorted," Walter assured him.

2

Dale laid a hand on the old man's supple shoulder. "I just hope all this work on our defenses won't be for nothing."

Once downstairs, Dale collected his Mossberg shotgun and an old army-surplus grenade satchel he'd purchased long ago for gardening but had since repurposed into an easy-access bag for his shotgun shells. By the time he pulled up the garage door, he could hear the approaching caravan of vehicles: a sound which sent a surge of nervous jitters up his spine. Brooke arrived and handed him one of the walkies. He kissed her forehead.

"Take care of her," he told Colton, who nodded in response. Colton then gave them a final good luck blessing before pulling the garage shut and locking it.

Dale, Sandy and Duke hurried past the pumphouse and the rows of planted vegetables and made it into the barn. Sandy was the first to climb the ladder into the loft. Dale followed, going up only far enough to hand her his rifle and shotgun before returning to scoop up Duke and repeat the process. His furry companion whined as Dale scaled the dozen rungs to the second level.

"It's all right, buddy," Dale told him. "We're almost there."

Sandy ran back to the opening in the floor and peered down at them in alarm. "You better hurry and get set up."

Dale reached the top at about the same time that the shooting started out front. So much of it was overlapping that he couldn't tell for sure how much was coming from the defenders inside and how much from the people trying to kill them.

The loft had a large set of doors which he and Sandy swung open. Laid out before the opening was a row of sandbags. It was a shooting position he'd prepared after the first assault by Randy's hired goons. Being up on the second story gave them the higher ground, which Walter had assured him was always an advantage during a gunfight, but there was something about the position which worried Dale and it was more than the fact that they were on their own. The wooden ladder they had used to reach the second level was built into the structure and couldn't be removed. Which meant that if any of Ortega's men made it into the barn the two of them would suddenly be facing a two-front war.

Sandy's only weapon was a single 9mm pistol for which she carried half a dozen magazines. For Dale's part, in addition to his shotgun and Remington hunting rifle, he was also equipped with his Ruger .45 caliber. That way, if Sandy's weapon ran out of ammo, he could always throw her his own pistol.

Dale set the barrel of his Remington on the sandbag before him. From here he would have a commanding view over anyone circling around either side of the house. But eyeing the heavy brush beyond the cleared edges of his property suddenly made him concerned. Like the retractable stairs and countless other projects, they simply hadn't had time to take care of everything.

"Too little, too late," he muttered under his breath as he worked the bolt, chambering a round. Just then the sound of gunfire coming from the front of the property grew sharply. Someone was getting hammered hard and Dale hoped to hell it was Ortega and his men.

•••

Edwardo Ortega

The cartel lieutenant watched from behind the engine block of his Escalade as the first wave of ten men

4

assaulted the house. The vehicles were parked sideways and arranged in a loose semi-circle to provide some cover and concealment. When Edwardo had arrived in Encendido he had done so with forty men by his side. He'd suffered a few losses during the biker ambush which had cut his forty down to thirty-four.

From here, Dale's property looked formidable, even if Edwardo wasn't prepared to say so out loud. The plan was simple. He and the others would provide covering fire from behind the barricade of vehicles while an initial group of ten men crossed the front lawn and made their way to the house. From there, they would use sledgehammers and shotguns to breach the walls. The rest of them would follow, overwhelming and killing everyone inside.

His enforcers were armed with a wide array of high-powered weaponry—HK G36s (5.56), AR-15s (.223), AK-74s (5.45 x 39mm), M4 Carbines (5.56)—more than enough to do what they'd come here for. Edwardo peered through the chaos of battle. Already, two men in the first wave had been wounded. A third was slumped forward on the front lawn, his foot caught in a booby trap, his body riddled with bullets. Rounds from a second-story window thudded into the windshield of the Escalade, forcing Edwardo to take cover.

Crouched next to him was El Grande, a burly three-hundred-and-fifty-pound enforcer. The two had met as children, El Grande a street kid who'd run messages as a courier for his own father, a lieutenant then in Fernando's burgeoning drug enterprise. Of course, that was before he'd gained the weight and won himself the name by which he was known today.

"These guys mean business," El Grande said, beads of sweat rolling down his obese face. His mouth was open and he was breathing hard like a man who'd been chasing after a frightened pig. "If we had a rocket launcher we could finish this in thirty seconds, I swear."

Edwardo didn't appreciate the suggestion. "Those two gringos said the place needs to be taken intact." He was referring to Sheriff Gaines and Mayor Reid. "Makes no sense even bothering if we can't get at the water."

Then came the loud impact of more incoming rounds, followed closely by the shriek of pain from a nearby man. To his left, one of the thugs clamped a hand over the side of his neck, blood squirting between his fingers. Edwardo snapped his thumb and index finger, ordering those nearby to attend to his wounds.

Taking casualties and caring for the wounded was something new for them. Back home, when a man was shot, he was usually left to fend for himself. There was no room in the organization for gimps or cripples. But they weren't at home anymore, were they? And because of that every man counted, wounded or not.

"The sheriff said we should drive them off the land," El Grande said, his eyes fixed on the bleeder a few feet away. "Avoid any unnecessary bloodshed. Sheriff said he'd given his word."

"What he promised isn't my concern," Edwardo replied. "They want this stubborn bastard off his land, want us to do their dirty work? Fine. But I'll do it my way."

Edwardo rose again, his rifle perched on the hood of the SUV, and rattled off a series of shots at that central window. The men around him came up and followed suit. He hoped to see that his enforcers had breached the wall already and were working their way inside. But the sight before him couldn't have been more different. Dead bodies sprawled on the lawn, a few still alive, screaming and clawing their way back toward the barricade of vehicles. Others had taken cover behind a row of sagebrush and juniper trees on the right flank,

6

their will to fight melting under the withering fire. The first wave hadn't just stalled, it had been chewed up and spat out.

Edwardo motioned for one of his subcommanders, a hardened warrior nicknamed El Ventrílocuo, the ventriloquist, on account of his legendary ability to get his torture victims talking. His muscular arms covered in tattoos, he had a scar running across his neck where someone had tried and failed to strangle him with a garrote.

"Take some men and circle around back," Edwardo told him. "There aren't enough gringos inside to cover every approach at once."

El Ventrílocuo grinned before pointing a crooked finger at nine men.

Edwardo and the others rose to provide covering fire.

Staying low, El Ventrílocuo's group moved along the row of sagebrush and gnarled desert trees, pushing toward the rear of the house.

Part of the problem was the concrete obstructions in the driveway which prevented them from bringing the vehicles closer. Edwardo surveyed the barbed-wire fence surrounding the front of the property. But that didn't mean there weren't other options. Edwardo waved over another subcommander and ordered him to take nine men and assault the front of the house while he, El Grande and two brothers stayed back to provide covering fire. If this didn't work, he had one more idea which was sure to do the trick.

•••

Colton and Dannyboy reached the top riser carrying two buckets of ammo apiece. They lowered the heavy containers onto the hardwood floor with a deep thud and a soft metallic jingle. While Walter had been the one to provide the vast majority of the rounds in their arsenal, none of them had taken the time to sort them by caliber. What had seemed little more than a nuisance was fast becoming a major problem.

No sooner had they set the buckets down than another volley of rounds fired from the cartel outside exploded through the walls, filling the air with bits of plaster and wood. Zach waved them forward.

"In here," he yelled. "And for God's sake keep your heads down or you're gonna lose 'em."

They took a deep breath and did as they were told. To their right was Dale's bedroom where Shane was crouched behind a row of sandbags, firing out the window. Brooke and Walter were positioned to the rear and side approaches respectively. Colton and Dannyboy were currently on ammo duty and acting as floaters, ready to jump in if someone was wounded or, worse, killed. Meanwhile Ann and Nicole were tasked with sorting rounds and replenishing spent magazines.

Zach handed Colton his AR and watched with pride as his son replaced him at the front window. The volume of fire coming at them from outside ebbed and flowed. Already Zach had two confirmed kills under his belt. And much of that had to do with the cartel's full-frontal assault, an insane strategy and one they had repulsed with relative ease. The barbed-wire fence and booby traps were also playing their part, helping to funnel the attackers into predesignated kill zones. At least, that was what the old geezer kept shouting whenever one of Ortega's men stumbled into a pitfall or one of those Apache foot traps. The sight would make Walter holler with joy, press his eye to the scope of his rifle and fire three rounds in quick succession.

"What'd I tell you?"

"Good shooting, old man," Zach told him. "But this ain't Korea, you know."

The wide grin on Walter's face said otherwise.

Now, with Colton and Dannyboy taking over, the change gave Zach a chance to check on the others. He went from room to room, ensuring everyone had enough ammo. He was heading toward Dale's room when Shane called out between three-round bursts. "I got a group heading around back," he shouted. "Five, maybe more. They're behind the underbrush and I couldn't get a clear shot."

Zach got on the walkie. "Dale, you're about to have some company on your left flank. Keep an eye on your ten o'clock."

Dale's staticky response came back a moment later. "Roger that."

Geez, Zach thought. *We're even starting to sound like army grunts.*

Still angling for a shot from the window, Shane was muttering. "If Dale had only listened to me, none of this would have happened."

"That may be so," Zach shot back. "But you don't negotiate with corrupt politicians. Stick your hand out and they're just as likely to bite it off. Believe me, I know."

Shane fired off two rounds before his AR clicked empty.

"Throw me a mag, will ya?"

Zach reached down, grabbed a full magazine and tossed it to him. A salvo of rounds thudded into the house, blasting out puffs of drywall. Through it all, Zach stood his ground, his eyes locked on Shane. He didn't like the guy. Didn't mean he wanted him dead or anything. Shane had just never passed the sniff test.

Crouched behind the sandbags, Shane stared back at him wide-eyed. "You sure have a death wish."

Zach grinned, crinkling the red rings around his eyes, remnants of surviving a bout of the H3N3. "I've been dead once already," he told Dale's brother. "Believe me, it's overrated."

The next flurry of bullets to impact the house was quickly followed by panicked shouts from the main defensive position, the one where Colton, Dannyboy and Walter were stationed.

"Bring the first-aid kit quick," a voice yelled over the din. "Someone's been hit."

Chapter 2
Dale

Dale spotted movement out among the sagebrush and juniper trees, fleeting glimpses of men as they ran through the undergrowth, and his body tensed. He had no reason to believe they'd made his position. And he could practically hear the soft quality of Walter's voice ringing in his head, laying out the enemy's strategy. Ortega was sending men around back looking for a point of weakness, a loose window board or a blind spot in the house's defenses. Something they could exploit in order to kill everyone inside.

He was sure Shane chalked up their current situation to Dale's refusal to share with his neighbors. It was an easy argument to make, especially when his younger brother seemed convinced all they needed to do was hand over a portion of their water and the bad guys would leave them alone. Perhaps that might have worked in the old days when the government, imperfect as it was, had at least been beholden to some form of public pressure and humiliation. But in this new world, devoid of newspapers, where public perception was almost entirely shaped by whether someone had access to a hot meal and something to wash it down with, things were far different.

Dale peered through the scope of his rifle, doing his best to follow the men as they hurried from right to left. Not only that, but the rules themselves had changed. More likely than not, the country had shrunk down into dozens of local, self-governing districts, like the fragmented state Italy had found itself in during the Renaissance. Without the shadow of some kind of centralized umbrella, each of these new independent districts would only be as safe or as productive as the local leaders could manage. A valley with wise and fair leadership might lie less than a handful of miles from a community run by a petty tyrant, eager to expand his sphere of influence at any cost. Unfortunately, Encendido had fallen under the latter, but Dale knew that given enough time and resources, even dictators could be overthrown.

"Are you gonna pull the trigger or not?" Sandy asked, a nervous furrow in her brow.

"Waiting for a clean shot," he told her. The men had stopped running and were hiding somewhere behind the chicken coop, among the trees and bushes, watching the house. One of them was ordered forward with a shout and soon emerged into the open. Dale settled the crosshairs over the man's chest and squeezed the trigger.

The rifle kicked back into his shoulder with a loud crack. The target's legs gave out and he collapsed into a dusty patch of earth. The others behind him began firing wildly, mostly at the house. While he didn't like putting those inside at risk, it was fine by Dale if these yahoos wanted to waste their ammo.

When the wild firing finally stopped, a handful of the cartel men behind the chicken coop fanned out and began to approach. Without a doubt there were more behind them, ready to spot the source of incoming rounds. Dale would have to be careful. Concealing muzzle flash was a lesson Walter hadn't taught him yet.

When they drew even with the pumphouse, Dale knew he had to act. A few of them were wearing bulletproof vests, but even that wouldn't do much to stop a 30-06 round from his Remington 700. A thug with a red bandana peered around the back corner of the pumphouse and Dale aimed the crosshairs for the center of his forehead. Dale steadied his breathing and squeezed the trigger. Another loud boom came as the man's head snapped back in a red mist.

The cartel members were firing again, but this time nearly all of it was aimed at the barn.

"They're onto us," Sandy said, her voice tight.

Duke let out a low growl.

"Easy, boy," Dale said, working the bolt and firing again at a man who was darting through the open. This time the shot went wide, kicking up a puff of powdery dust. He chambered another, fired and it also went wide. These guys were moving too fast.

Sandy opened up with her pistol, letting off a handful of rounds. Then shots from the treeline thudded into the sandbags, forcing both of them to stay low.

"If they keep us pinned down, we're as good as dead," Dale told her.

Sandy looked worried and headed over to the ladder and the hole in the floor.

Dale got on the walkie. "Zach, we got multiple bogeys around the barn. We could use some support back here."

He waited for a reply, each second feeling like an hour as bullets whizzed over his head. Dale popped up with the Remington, trying to acquire a target. To the right of the chicken coop, lying prone behind a piñon tree, was the exposed left thigh of a cartel member. If he

13

could hit the target, the shot might not kill the man, but it would at least take him out of the fight. Dale squeezed the trigger and watched the man's jeans ripple, followed by a bellow of pain. From here, it looked like the round had snapped his femur in two.

Behind him, he heard Sandy lay off a half-dozen rounds with her 9mm. She was shooting down through the hole. The cartel members below returned fire, sending bullets bursting through the floorboards, tossing splinters into the air. Sandy shrieked with pain and rolled out of the way. The blood in Dale's veins froze with terror. He grabbed his shotgun and rushed over to where Sandy had been standing. The cartel men below must have thought she was alone, because one of them was scaling the ladder. Dale aimed the barrel at his face and fired. The weapon let out a deafening roar as the thug was thrown to the ground in a heap. Racking the shotgun again, he let off three more shots, firing through the floor, trying to wound or kill anyone standing beneath him.

Quickly, he then made his way to Sandy. Her face was cut from the flying bits of sharpened wood.

"Are you hit?" he asked, checking her for an entry wound.

"I don't think so," she replied, her cloudy eyes looking over his shoulder. Suddenly, she raised her pistol and it clicked empty. Another cartel member had just cleared the second floor and was shifting to raise the pistol in his free hand.

Dale struggled to swing the heavy shotgun around in time. The look of bloodlust in the man's eyes was clear. He was muscular with a scar on his neck. Dale had killed his friends and now this monster was about to return the favor.

Dale managed to rack the shotgun right as Duke pounced, clamping his powerful jaws around the thug's wrist, shaking his head violently. The man let out a yelp of agony as he let go of the ladder. Duke lurched forward, struggling to hold onto the weight of the man's falling body, but it was a tug of war the eighty-five-pound dog was bound to lose. If Duke didn't release him, Duke would fall too and be at the mercy of any of the others still down there. Duke's paws were close to the edge, his body drawn back, the muscles in his haunches and neck bunched up like tight cords.

"Release," Dale shouted and the dog complied, licking his lips as the man fell. Shots from downstairs followed the man's hard landing, barely missing Duke. The dog recoiled, looking left and right, unsure what was happening.

"Heel," Dale ordered. That was when he heard the walkie come to life and the sound of fire coming from the house.

Dale went to the sandbags and saw Colton and Dannyboy opening up from the back window on the men in the barn and others scattered around the rear of the property. Zach's silhouette was between them, surveying the situation and pointing out targets.

"Keep running, you bastards!" Zach shouted over the walkie.

"Appreciate the help," Dale replied. "Things were a little touch-and-go here for a while. Everyone inside safe?"

There was a delay in Zach's response and it drew shivers up Dale's spine. "Zach, is anyone hurt?"

"We've all taken a hit in one way or another," he replied. "Some worse than others."

Dale swallowed. "Was anyone…" His voice trailed off.

Zach started to respond, but was cut off by a thundering boom.

"The hell was that?" Dale said.

15

No response.

"Zach, what's going on over there?" The panic ran through Dale's body like a virus.

He glared at the walkie, willing it to deliver an explanation. The only response came across the yard from the house itself in the form of muffled automatic gunfire. It sounded as though a gun battle was going on within the house. Then came that sickening feeling as Dale understood. The cartel had found a way inside.

Chapter 3

"We have to go and now," Dale told Sandy, who was sitting on the floor, pistol in hand, keeping an eye on the loft opening.

"Whatever that was, it sounded like a bomb went off," she said, rising quickly to her feet.

"They've breached the lower level," he told her, leaving the Remington resting against the row of sandbags. "There's no time to lose."

But even in his frantic state, Dale knew well enough not to go charging into danger. Just because Colton and Dannyboy had scattered Ortega's men in the back of the house didn't mean that the bad guys had gone very far.

"I'll head down first," he told her, "and let you know if it's clear."

Shouldering his Mossberg, Dale drew his Ruger .45 and quickly descended the ladder, swiveling as soon as he could, to check for threats. He reached the bottom and scanned any hiding places inside the barn, searching behind piles of plywood, spools of chicken wire and barbed wire and a host of useless junk he'd been meaning to get rid of for years.

Satisfied the barn was clear, Dale went back and got Duke, Sandy not far behind.

They exited the barn, Dale and Sandy holding their pistols in the ready position. The sharp report of automatic fire ringing through the open second-story windows made it clear the gun battle going on inside was a fierce one.

Additional shots rang out, but these sounded different. He and Sandy were on the right of the house when bullets thudded into the wood siding. They spun at the same time, each aiming their weapon. Two cartel members had come from behind the barn. One had a rifle, the other a pistol, his right arm mangled and dangling by his side. He must have been the one Duke had bitten on the ladder.

Dale rolled left and opened fire. Sandy dropped to one knee and did the same. Woodchips exploded from the front of the barn as shots failed to hit their mark. Dale emptied his magazines as the cartel members fired back.

With two bullets remaining, Sandy struck the man with the rifle, dropping him to the ground like a sack of dirty laundry. The sight made the other man flee back behind the barn. He was shooting from his left hand, likely not the one he was most comfortable with, which explained why he'd decided to tuck tail.

Dale and Sandy changed magazines and headed toward the front of the house, staying low as they approached, in case more of Ortega's men were by the road.

But that didn't seem to be the case. There were a few shots coming from a group of vehicles fifty yards away, but most of the firing was coming from inside.

Glancing from right to left, Dale spotted a clear set of tire tracks leading from a gaping hole in the fence by the road toward the boarded-up front entrance. The pickup had plowed into the house right up to the windshield, its tail lights on, the engine running, the back wheels still spinning. The impact had torn a gaping hole large enough for Ortega's remaining men to storm through. On the plus side, the holes they'd dug for booby traps seemed to have slowed the truck's momentum enough to prevent it from doing far more damage.

Dale holstered his pistol and came up with the shotgun. Sandy and Duke were on his six as they stayed low and headed through the hole and into the darkened confines of the house.

Dale's eyes struggled to adjust. They'd left a bright, sunny world and entered a darkened hellscape. The whiff of gasoline and cordite was strong. So too was the noise, weapons of every caliber rattling off in every direction. With the windows and doors all boarded up, it was difficult to see more than five feet in front of you. To their right, near the kitchen, Dale could hear the sound of men crying out in pain. A voice from the darkness called to him.

"El Ventrílocuo, is that you?"

"Yes," Dale replied and opened fire. The light from the exploding end of his barrel lit the terrified thug's face before he was thrown back by the blast. Dale racked the shotgun, following the sound of gunfire. Two more cartel members were working their way up the staircase by the kitchen. They turned right as Dale and Sandy fired. Both men froze in a strange tableau of death before slumping forward. Climbing the stairs, Dale called out so they wouldn't get shot by their own side.

"Watch out," a voice that might have been Brooke's shouted back.

A gunman stepped out from one of the bedrooms with an AR-15 and managed to get a shot off before

19

Dale fed his chest some buckshot. The rifle flew from the man's hands. When Dale reached the top of the stairs he spotted two cartel members jumping from the window in his bedroom.

Dale headed back into the hallway to help clear the rest of the second floor. "I'm coming through," he said. "Don't shoot."

Zach emerged from one of the bedrooms, aiming a pistol. He lowered it when he was certain it was Dale. "They had us pinned down," he explained with noticeable frustration.

"It's not over yet," Dale chided his brother-in-law. "There may be more of them." He peered into the guest bedroom which faced onto the road and saw Dannyboy lying on the floor with a bloodstained pillowcase wrapped around his head. Next to him was Walter, struggling to draw in shallow breaths. Ann was tending to both Dannyboy and Walter. Nicole was kneeling next to her, sobbing.

Dale swore.

"He was one of the first to get hit," Zach told him, referring to Walter. "Crazy old man thinks he's Rambo or something."

"Will he be okay?"

Zach shrugged. "Hey, I'm no doctor, I just play one on TV."

More shots from outside.

He thought about Brooke and Colton. "Is everyone else accounted for?" Dale asked.

From a bedroom at the other end of the hall they both emerged, looking exhausted and shell-shocked.

"Where's Shane?" Dale asked. But the blank expressions on everyone's faces told him nobody knew.

"He was positioned in your room. Spent most of his time complaining," Zack said. "Things were going well until the whole house shook. After that everything just went haywire."

Dale, Zach, Sandy and Duke ran to where Shane had been shooting, stepping over the dead body at the doorway. There they found Dale's room was empty. Scooping up the cartel member's AR, Dale went to the window and began scanning outside. A shot zinged over his head and he took cover. But he'd seen enough. In the distance, the cartel were loading the wounded and beginning to retreat. Bodies lay strewn around the small part of the property he could see, but in all of that carnage, Shane was nowhere to be found.

The next few minutes were spent sweeping the interior of the house to ensure all the cartel members were either dead or gone. Once that was done, Dale ordered sentries to cover every approach while he, Zach and Duke searched for Shane. Ducking through the large hole in the wall, Dale moved to reach into the pickup to turn off the ignition when he saw a body slumped over the passenger seat. The windshield above the wheel was cracked and stained with blood where the driver's head must have struck upon impact.

"Serves you right," Dale said, killing the engine with a flick of his wrist. Three more bodies lay on the front lawn, their feet stuck in traps, their torsos riddled with bullet holes. Others were visible on the driveway, cut down as the first wave had been beaten back. It must have been an especially brutal assault, especially for those facing Walter's aged, but experienced hands.

An eerie silence descended over the whole area, leaving Dale with a strange and saddened mix of emotions. He was relieved that, bloody and battered, they hadn't been completely overrun and at the same time devastated that his brother was missing and his mentor critically injured. It was a high price to pay, but he couldn't be more proud.

Zach returned from the rear of the property.

"Any sign of him?" Dale asked, holding tight to the last threads of hope.

Zach shook his head. "He just up and vanished."

"I doubt that very much," Dale replied. "They got him, which might be why they were in such a hurry to pull back."

"You thinking they're gonna use him as a bargaining chip?"

"In some ways I hope so," Dale replied. "Because the alternative is that he's already dead."

A shout from inside the house sent them scurrying inside. Brooke was in the kitchen, holding the remains of a bloodstained calendar. It looked as though a wounded cartel member had ripped it off the wall and run a bloody hand across the front. But the closer Dale looked, the more those bloody streaks began to take on the appearance of letters and words.

You have one hour to leave or he's dead.

Chapter 4

"He's being held hostage," Dale told the others, holding up the bloody calendar as proof. They were gathered upstairs to figure out what to do next.

Still kneeling in prayer beside her wounded father, Nicole dissolved into tears. Ann rubbed her back reassuringly and tried to tell her it would be all right.

Zach stuffed the pistol into the seat of his pants. "Can't say I'm Shane's biggest fan, but seems to me we're wasting time squawking like a bunch of mother hens when we should be mounting a rescue operation."

"That's exactly what Sheriff Gaines and Mayor Reid will be expecting," Dale shot back.

Zach was surprised by his quick answer. "How do you figure?"

Colton, who had been staring out the window, keeping watch, turned to his father. "They kidnapped Sandy a few days back. Dale, Shane and I had to go rescue her."

Zach eyed Sandy up and down. "Kidnapped? Honey, you don't look like a kid to me."

Sandy ignored him.

23

Dale felt his hands tighten into fists. "This isn't helping. Colton's right. They knew if they took one of us, we'd be tempted to mount another rescue. For all we know, this was part of their plan. If they failed to kill us, then they would grab someone and use that person as leverage."

"If we stay and do nothing, then Shane dies," Zach said, making no bones about how he felt. "He's your brother, man."

"I get that," Dale said, not liking Zach's tone. "But if half of us leave to try to rescue Shane, we may be leaving ourselves overly exposed, especially with a giant hole punched into the front of the house. Even at full strength we were barely able to hold them off."

"There must be at least ten bodies out there," Zach said pointedly. "Many of the others who got away won't be fighting anytime soon."

Dale crossed his arms over his chest. "So what are you saying?"

"I'm telling you we have an advantage and we should not let it go to waste."

"What about the sheriff and his deputies?" Colton threw in, shrinking when he saw the look of displeasure in his father's face.

"Colton's right," Dale said, pacing back and forth and running his fingers through his hair. "We may be playing right into their hands. Running straight into a trap."

"I vote we do what they say," Nicole moaned, struggling to get the words out.

Even Ann was surprised by that. "But where will we go? What will we do for food and shelter?"

"We can go back to our old place," Nicole told her, rising to her feet. "I'll start getting my things together."

"No one's going anywhere," Dale told her. "You left your house for a reason, Nicole." Dale stopped and drew

24

in a deep breath. "Listen, I get that our emotions are running high. I want Shane back just as much as the rest of you, but putting everyone at risk over one person's safety isn't a smart move. If your father were conscious, I'm sure he'd be the first to agree with me."

Nicole stood, frozen with disbelief. "I can't believe you're being so cold," she hissed. "It's fine for you to condemn my husband to death. Would you be sitting back if it was Brooke's life on the line?"

The sting of her words made Dale physically recoil. The emotional part of him wanted to tell her to keep quiet, that she was making a difficult situation even worse, but another part of him realized she did have a point. What if Brooke had been in Shane's place? Would he be mulling over the most practical options? Or would he already be out the door, his Mossberg and Remington by his side with Duke riding shotgun? Frightening as it was to even contemplate such a scenario, Dale was thankful she hadn't been the one taken.

Then on the heels of that thought came something worse. What if she had been the real target? The one person who Sheriff Gaines knew possessed the power to short-circuit Dale's ability to think straight and do what was best for the group. The possibility was far too frightening to contemplate and far too plausible to ignore.

While the two most obvious choices would only place them in greater danger, there was a third option they hadn't yet considered.

Dale cleared his throat and began telling them what was on his mind. "Maybe it's time we reach out and give them what they want."

Brooke's eyes grew wide. "Hey, I've been preaching diplomacy since all of this began, but you said if we gave these guys a single drop they wouldn't stop until they had it all."

"I did," Dale admitted. "And trust me, this isn't what I want. But we're not in a position to choose between good and bad options. We're at a fork in the road and every path leads somewhere bad. I'm just trying to figure out which one will keep the rest of us alive."

"So what do we do?" Sandy asked.

"We draft a note and begin negotiations," Dale said. "Like two punch-drunk heavyweights, both sides have been bruised and battered. If we're going to ever get decent terms, it may be now."

"I'd like to write it," Brooke offered, her eyes already staring off into empty space as she considered the words she would use.

"Okay. I'll go over it when you're done," Dale said. "But first we'll need to make sure Shane's still alive." Nicole's features crumpled at the very suggestion before Dale went on. "Only after will we offer a set amount of water each week."

"You're making a mistake trying to negotiate with these animals," Zach told him. "I know the way these cartel types think. I've done time with them. In their minds, diplomacy is no different than admitting weakness and if there's one thing they hate, it's weakness."

"That may be," Dale replied. "But we won't be negotiating with *them*. We'll be talking with Sheriff Gaines and Mayor Reid. Ortega and his drug-dealing associates don't belong in this country, let alone in this community, and I intend to send them packing the moment I get the chance."

Sandy checked her watch. "Then we better hurry. There isn't much time."

26

Chapter 5

While Brooke worked frantically on a draft of the letter for Sheriff Gaines and Mayor Reid, Dale and most of the others began clearing away the dead.

Ann and Nicole stayed upstairs with Walter and Dannyboy. The old man was having a difficult time breathing. The women were doing everything they could to keep him alive. They'd stopped the bleeding, but they suspected he'd suffered a collapsed lung when the bullet had torn through the right side of his chest. He would have to be monitored and seen by a doctor if at all possible.

Dale's first order of business was to back the cartel's pickup out from the house and park it over near the pumphouse.

With weapons slung over their shoulders, Dale and Sandy then began carrying the dead from inside the house, laying them in piles. Zach and Colton worked around back doing the same. It was grim and depressing work and not the first time they'd been in a position to stack up the dead like so much cordwood. Dale was starting to feel like an undertaker. He'd be lying if he didn't admit a few of them were still clinging to life, but that wasn't anything a well-placed bullet couldn't fix.

In thirty minutes from now, they would be expected to vacate the property. And with every second that ticked away, the pressure to save his brother's life was mounting. He could feel it churning his insides, working his gut in an uncomfortable, almost sickening way. Still, he felt it was best not to let on what an agonizing decision it had been. In spite of the differences between him and his brother, Shane was blood and deserved every reasonable action to ensure his safety. The real question was, how could any responsible person jeopardize the safety of those in his charge for a single life? It was a conundrum that had likely challenged folks throughout history.

Sandy grunted as they tossed one of the bodies onto the front lawn. Like the men, the grass was yellow and devoid of life. From around back they could hear Zach and Colton engaged in what sounded like a jovial conversation.

"They seem to be making up for lost time," Sandy observed, stopping long enough to fan herself with the straw cowboy hat she was wearing.

Dale took in what she said. "I guess right about now I can't find anything worth laughing about."

Sandy stopped, removed her gloves and touched his arm. The soft pads of her fingers felt nice against his skin.

"Don't take it to heart, Dale. Not everyone deals with trauma in the same way."

A cup of water was resting on the steps between them and Dale drank from it, offering some to Sandy, which she gladly accepted. "Believe me," he told her, "it takes more than that to ruffle my feathers."

"You're upset he called you out in front of the others."

"I won't lie, it did sting," he admitted. "I'd do anything for Shane."

"I know you would. But you also know the way Zach is."

Dale nodded, took the cup back and set it on the stairs. "Far as I see it, that's the problem. He and I are like oil and water. Put us in a bottle and mix real well, you'd think we were simpatico, but before long both parts start pulling apart from one another."

"I see what you mean," Sandy said, looking thoughtful. "Maybe you could talk to him."

Dale laughed. "This isn't Dr. Phil, Sandy. Right or wrong, that's not how men work. We don't sit down and have a heart-to-heart and talk out our differences."

"Why not?"

Dale started back for the house and stopped. "Beats me. Ask that short little guy who wrote *Men are from Mars, Women are from Neptune*."

Sandy couldn't help but giggle. "Venus. Women are from Venus."

"You know what I mean."

"You know, my mother never once told me to my face that she loved me," Sandy said and Dale furrowed his brow, wondering where she was going with this. "I knew it, I suppose in the way kids know lots of stuff adults neglect to tell them. I also knew she was lonely in the years after my father died. She'd always claim she was too old to start chasing after men and too tired to worry about whether they wanted to be chased in the first place. Became something of a mantra for her. But in spite of a child's intuition, it wasn't until after she passed and I had to sort through her things that I realized how little of her I really knew. She was a knockout when she was young, probably beating the boys back with a stick."

"I see where you get it from."

Sandy grinned. "That's when I found a bunch of letters she'd written me, but never mailed. There was one for every major turning point in my life, when I graduated from high school and then college, and later when I was hired by the sheriff's office."

"What were the letters about?"

"She was telling me how proud she was and how much she loved me. I was too young to help her bridge that gap, to overcome whatever was keeping her from expressing how she felt. My point is that sometimes you gotta be the one to reach out, even if it's not your responsibility. Sometimes you gotta be the adult."

Brooke appeared in the gaping hole by the front entrance. She was holding a handwritten piece of paper.

"It's done," she said, proud and somewhat relieved.

Dale went over and read it.

To Sheriff Gaines and Mayor Reid,

We received your ransom note and have considered your offer. Here is our response. To leave our property and the security it affords us would accomplish nothing apart from placing everyone here in grave danger.

Too much blood has already been spilled. Can't we set aside our differences and work together to stop this senseless carnage? The people of Encendido are thirsty and we're willing to share some of our water with the town, but we have a few conditions. Before any of that, we need proof that Shane is still alive. Once that's been established, then we can set up a time and place to discuss terms.

When he was done, Dale folded the letter and placed it in the envelope. "Well done, Brooke." His lips were curled into a smile, even though he couldn't help but wonder whether he was starting down that slippery slope he'd feared from the very beginning. He turned to Sandy. "Get on the radio to the sheriff's office and tell him if he wants our answer he'll find it by the mesquite tree across the street."

She nodded and moved past them, disappearing into the house.

"Do you think it'll work?" Brooke asked, her large brown eyes lacking the innocence they'd once possessed.

Dale pulled her in close. "Sheriff Gaines may not be a good man, but he isn't unreasonable." Even as the words passed his lips, Dale struggled to believe they were true.

Chapter 6

Everyone was inside when the pickup raced down the long dusty road. Dale watched from the front window while Colton, Zach and Brooke scanned the other avenues of approach to ensure they weren't falling for some sort of distraction. Although the truck's windows were tinted, Dale knew well enough the vehicle belonged to Ortega or one of his men. They'd searched for the cartel lieutenant's body among the dead and had found no sign of him.

The truck backed up until it was parallel with the tree. The passenger door swung open and closed just as quickly before the pickup sped off, a swirling cloud trailing behind it. Seemed the other side was equally worried about falling prey to an ambush. There were still fifteen minutes before the hour was up. With any luck, they might begin negotiations before the sun went down.

Walter was lying on the bed next to Dale, his shirt peeled off, his chest wrapped with bloodstained bandages. Always attentive, Ann was by his side, holding his hand.

"He still out?" Dale asked, standing near the window. The old man's chest was rising and falling in a steady, albeit weak rhythm.

Ann turned, looking up at him, a dreadfully worried expression on her face. "I've been telling him to hold on."

Dale leaned over and rubbed her thin back. Her ribs were prominent, making it feel like he was running his hand over a washboard.

"Mind if I have a word with him?"

Ann stood and placed Walter's hand by his side. "Of course." She left the room, her delicate footfalls like those of a ghost.

Dale settled into the seat, listening to the creak as it settled under his weight. He glanced down at his own hands. There was blood on his fingers and he wondered who it might have belonged to.

"I heard you fought well today," he told the old man. "I'm not sure you can even hear me. But I wanted to say I can't thank you enough for everything you've done to keep us safe." Dale laughed. "I can almost hear what you'd say, that you were only doing your part, but without you we probably wouldn't have… Well, let's just say the situation would have turned out different. Stay strong, my friend. We need you."

When he was done, Dale said a prayer, asking for Walter to be healed, but also asking for the wisdom and the strength to do what was right.

An hour passed with still no word from the other side about their offer. They'd used the time to bring large pieces of plywood from the barn to the front of the house, where they nailed them in place to cover the hole left by the pickup. From the inside, they added additional two-by-fours to brace and strengthen the repair work. Strong as it might be, it would never stop another truck

33

from crashing into the house. That project would come later, once the current business with Randy and Hugh Reid was over and done with.

But with every second that passed, Dale grew more and more impatient, more and more nervous. He saw himself hopping into his pickup and racing into town, armed to the teeth, on a one-way mission to take down as many of them as he could before he was finally stopped. Somewhere his brother was being held and perhaps even tortured. There was nothing Dale could do about that and the knowledge was driving him nuts.

Just then, Colton called from the second floor. The pickup was back. Dale sprinted up the stairs two at a time and raced into the front bedroom. The others were already there and Dale struggled to see what was happening. Would they leave a note of their own designed to open the negotiations or would they simply drop Shane off as a sign of goodwill?

"Oh, my God," Sandy said, the nails of her right hand digging into the window sill.

The truck was about even with the property when Dale saw what looked like a department store mannequin set on fire and kicked out the back of the truck. It rolled several times, thudding against one of the barbed-wire posts, black and orange flames licking several feet into the air.

Nicole's hands were clasped over her open mouth, shuttering a horrific scream trapped deep inside. Colton rattled off a handful of futile shots at the fleeing vehicle from the AR. Almost hypnotically, Dale's gaze swiveled back to the fence post, itself on fire, before he understood that what he was seeing. Horrifying as it was, this was no dream, nor was it a department store mannequin the cartel had tossed from the bed of that pickup.

It was his brother Shane's dead body.

Chapter 7

Dale raced from the house, fire extinguisher in hand, leaping instinctively over the remaining booby traps as he raced toward the flaming mass that was once Shane. He doused the fire, searching immediately for any semblance of life. His brother's body was naked, every corner of flesh blackened. In many parts, the skin, sprinkled with copious amounts of fine white powder from the extinguisher, had melted into an amorphous mass.

Nicole was running toward them when Dale held up a hand, telling her to stay away. When she didn't comply, Zach and Colton grabbed her by the arms and held her back as she shrieked in frustration and anguish. This was no way to see your loved one, especially for the last time.

"Get her out of here," Dale shouted, scooping up his brother's still-sizzling body. When they'd managed to coax Nicole back to the house, Dale carried Shane to the garage. Sandy and Ann cleared a work bench where Dale could set his brother's body down. Thin tendrils of smoke rose from the blackened flesh. The sleeves of Dale's shirt were speckled with strips of his brother's skin, but he didn't care. There was no longer any doubt that his brother was dead.

"Can you wash and prep him for burial?" he asked Ann, his voice quiet, toneless.

Colton came up behind him, looking somber and still clearly in a state of shock. "I'll start digging a hole, I guess."

"Thank you," Dale said, almost robotically. Mercifully, the full weight of what had just happened hadn't sunk in yet. That would come later. He entered the house, went up to his bedroom and grabbed his pistol and shotgun as well as his Remington. Somewhere nearby he could hear Nicole sobbing uncontrollably. In the span of a few hours she'd lost her husband and was at risk of losing her father too.

Dale came back through the garage as Ann and Sandy were beginning the grim task of cleaning Shane's body. He stopped briefly to glance down at what had once been his brother's handsome face and was now little more than a melted wax dummy. Duke was by his master's side, looking melancholy himself, perhaps sensing on some unknowable level the terrible loss they'd just suffered.

Sandy noticed the weapons he was carrying. "Tell me you're not about to do something stupid."

"Maybe Zach was right," Dale said. "It was dumb to think these animals could be reasoned with. They aren't human, Sandy. Someone needs to put them down."

"Dale," she shouted. "You're only going to get yourself killed. At least take Zach and Colton along."

Dale's eyes fell to Duke, sitting obediently by his side. "This isn't your fight either, buddy," he told the German shepherd. "You stay here and protect the others."

Duke barked and it sounded to Dale almost like a protest.

He walked away and Duke tried to follow. "Stay," Dale yelled.

Duke's ears peeled back as he lowered himself to the ground, whining.

The pickup that had smashed into their front door was parked out back. Dale got in and maneuvered the vehicle down the driveway and past the obstacles. In the rear view, he caught a glimpse of Sandy and the worried expression on her face.

Once he drew nearer to the center of town, Dale cut off the main thoroughfare and took the back roads. A right onto Columbo Street, followed by a left on Enterprise Way. His first order of business was to kill Mayor Reid. Afterward, he would deal with Sheriff Gaines. And if his luck hadn't run out by then, he would take out Ortega and as many cartel men as he could. If he didn't make it back, at least he would have helped rid Encendido and the world of the kind of scum that were only capable of spreading hate and misery.

Up until this point, Dale had fought hard to keep to himself, to weather the storm and do what he needed to keep his family safe. To those who were willing to trade fairly, he'd been more than happy to share what he had. But some men didn't have a conscience. Some men couldn't be reasoned with. To their kind justice and freedom were four-letter words.

The kidnapping of his brother had put him in a terrible position, one which had forced Dale to choose between losing a lot or losing a little. After the cartel men had picked up their letter, he'd somehow managed to convince himself he'd found a way everyone could come out on top. All they needed was to hammer out the finer details. Shane would come home and the price to pay would be nothing more than a few thousand gallons of water. It hadn't mattered to him at the time that there were no more courts to help keep men like Mayor Reid from going back on their word. At the end of the day, in a world without the rule of law, if a man didn't have his word, he didn't have anything at all.

Abandoned houses whipped by on either side of him as Dale sped along the back roads toward the Teletech plant. He pulled the truck into a driveway rife with weeds and neglect, killing the ignition and loading up with weapons and ammo as he listened to the engine tick down.

He slung the Mossberg over his shoulder. The pistol he put in the holster on his hip. But the Remington he kept in his hands. He would find a nice secluded spot somewhere within a hundred yards of the plant's main entrance and there he would wait for his target to approach.

This was Mayor Reid's preferred haunt, even more so after word had begun to circulate that Edwardo Ortega had evicted him from his own mansion. If Reid hadn't realized he'd made a big fat mistake by laying out the welcome mat for Ortega and his crew beforehand, surely he had then.

Cutting through a backyard, Dale caught sight of Teletech looming in the distance. He walked for another ten minutes before finding what he thought was the perfect spot on a knoll sprinkled with wild grass and shrubs. He lowered himself onto the hot, dusty ground, using a large rock and some torn leaves as a shooting platform. The rifle was loaded and zeroed in. All he needed to do now was wait. Already the sun was low in the sky, kissing the mountain range to the west with tinges of oranges and yellows.

For almost fifteen minutes, the grounds around the factory were deathly still. In the distance every so often came the sound of gunfire. Most of it seemed to be coming from the far side of town. It was sporadic, which told him it wasn't a firefight. It sounded more like a house-clearing operation.

Dale was still contemplating his next move when three Escalades pulled up to the factory. The second SUV pulled alongside the first, cutting off Dale's immediate view of who had arrived in the lead vehicle. He watched through his scope as the crests of men's heads moved just beyond view. Could one of them be Ortega? The thought was a tantalizing one, although Dale worried about having his hopes dashed.

Soon, the large factory doors peeled back and a handful of figures emerged from inside. Six deputies along with Sheriff Gaines and Mayor Reid. They walked up to the group of cartel men who were still just out of sight. When the deputies came to a stop, three of them were blocking any shot he had at either the sheriff or the mayor. Dale swore. He had a choice: either reposition and risk being detected by anyone near the plant who happened to be scanning the desert, or wait a little bit longer. He took a deep breath to calm his clip-clopping heart. They had to break off eventually and if the sun hadn't completely set by then, Dale would have his shot.

Peering through the scope, he watched as a heated conversation took shape. The deputies were on edge. They seemed afraid. Dale assumed from their unease that the sheriff and Mayor Reid were talking to Ortega, discussing the cartel's failed attempt to evict them and take over his property. Mayor Reid, normally calm and collected, was shouting, flinging his arms over his head, clearly upset. Perhaps Ortega was trying to pin the failure on him somehow. Perhaps the drug lieutenant was suggesting if Gaines and all of his deputies had come along for the ride things might have turned out differently.

Now it was the sheriff's turn to talk and he appeared far more controlled, a counterpoint to his agitated boss. Dale imagined he was telling Ortega that he'd wanted all the glory for himself and should have included them in the attack. Of course all of this was speculation as Dale's mind worked feverishly to read everyone's body language. His index finger was next to the trigger, tapping the side of the rifle. He had to be ready for those three idiots to move. Then he could take the first step toward finishing this mess once and for all.

For a brief moment, Dale's mind wandered to the numbness creeping into his legs before he realized that the scene before him had suddenly changed. The shouting had grown louder as two of the deputies took unsteady steps backward. The others dropped their hands to their service pistols. Ortega emerged from behind one of the black Escalades, a silver Desert Eagle in the grip of his extended right hand. Perhaps instinctively, Mayor Reid's hands flew into the air in surrender. He seemed to be pleading with Ortega, trying to placate the man. Dale saw the large silver pistol kick back in Ortega's hand a split second before the actual sound of it firing hit his ears. Mayor Reid's head snapped back, his arms pinwheeling as his body struck the ground, kicking up a fine puff of beige particles.

Dale couldn't believe his eyes. Ortega had beaten him to the punch and done Dale's work for him. So why wasn't Dale filled with elation rather than dread?

Ortega's men surged forward, leveling automatic weapons. The deputies threw their hands up, all except for Sheriff Gaines. Maybe Ortega was going to finish him off too. But Dale's hopes were dashed when the deputies lowered their hands and dragged the mayor's body away. The sight was so surreal, it took Dale a few seconds to realize he had a clear shot at Gaines. His finger found the trigger at about the same time the sheriff began walking back toward the giant Teletech doors.

"Now or never," Dale told himself. *Remember what the old man said. Slow your breathing and always give a moving target a slight lead.* In another few seconds, the sheriff would be gone. Dale squeezed the trigger and watched the bullet arc out from the barrel and thud into the dirt at Gaines' feet.

He swore and worked the bolt. Sticking his eye back to the scope, he saw with that single miss, everything had shifted once again. Sheriff Gaines had taken cover behind a parked car, his men pointing in Dale's direction, shouting at the cartel men near the three Escalades. They were pointing out Dale's position.

The first black SUV hit the gas, heading straight for him, bumping wildly over the rough terrain. The other two quickly followed suit.

That can't be good, Dale chastised himself. With blood pounding in his ears, he hopped to his feet and collected his weapons. Rounds fired by the deputies and the cartel men in the SUVs thudded into the ground around him. His legs pumping furiously, Dale raced back toward the truck, not entirely sure whether he would make it.

Chapter 8

The gnarled mesquite trees acted as sentries, slowing the progress of the oncoming SUVs. Sweating profusely in the final threads of late-afternoon sun, Dale hoofed it along the trail, struggling to maintain his footing over the uneven ground. Right now, a twisted ankle would be just as fatal as a bite from a rattlesnake, both of which were distinct possibilities. Rounds tore up the ground on either side of him as the men below continued to fire in the hopes that a lucky shot would find its mark. Then a loud ping of metal on metal sounded as a bullet ricocheted off the Mossberg slung over his back. He had briefly considered dropping the shotgun to keep it from weighing him down and now it seemed he'd made the right choice keeping it.

By the time he crested the hill into the neighborhood where he had parked the pickup, the shooting had stopped. Glancing over his shoulder, he also noticed the black SUV's were gone.

Have they given up? he wondered. More likely, Ortega and his posse were going to try to cut off his escape.

Breathing hard, Dale finally reached the truck. He gave a quick scan for threats before he hopped inside, pushing the weapons onto the seat next to him. With a turn of his wrist he started the vehicle and backed out. The drive home wouldn't take more than a few minutes. If all went well, he'd be back behind the relative safety of the fortress walls before Ortega had a chance to swing around.

Dale pressed the gas, white-knuckling the steering wheel as he screeched around a corner. Cesare Avenue was a long, relatively straight street which led south past the high school and onto Charleston. That way lay his house and safety. His spirits were beginning to brighten when three black SUVs came swinging onto Cesare, racing toward him. They were a hundred yards away when Dale reached over, buckled his seatbelt and accelerated.

The SUVs did the same.

"So they wanna play chicken," Dale growled, pressing the pedal all the way down. Houses flicked past him on the right. On the left, Encendido High's football field was coming into view.

The second SUV swung into the oncoming lane, leaving Dale with two choices: a head-on collision or the ditch.

They were less than twenty yards away when he slammed the brake hard and spun the wheel to the left. The back tires screeched, belching out white smoke and the smell of searing rubber. The nose of Dale's pickup jerked left. Cutting across the road, he shot forward onto the football field, narrowly missing the oncoming SUVs.

Dale hollered the way a daredevil might after narrowly escaping a brush with death. Behind him, the SUVs had swung around and were also cutting across the football field.

The sight ahead of him made Dale's gut seize up. The school parking lot was mostly empty, except for a clump of abandoned cars. The only way through the mess was a four-foot gap between two sedans. He was either going to crash or give both sides of the truck a very close shave.

As if to remind him he wasn't alone, the cartel men began shooting again, a few of the shots striking his tailgate. One took out the mirror on the passenger side.

If the drivers of the SUVs hadn't seen what was coming by now, it was too late. Dale braced himself as he aimed his pickup right for the opening. The impact was sudden and incredibly loud as the squeal of metal gave way to a burst of sparks. The truck burst through and fishtailed as Dale fought to maintain control. Roaring through the parking lot, he caught a glimpse in his rear-view as two of the three SUVs braked hard while the third t-boned one of the abandoned sedans, the back end rising several feet into the air before crashing back to earth.

Dale didn't let up his frantic pace until he was home. Slowing down at last, he pulled into his property and navigated around the concrete obstacles. He glanced down and saw that his hands were shaking. He brought the truck to a spot between the pumphouse and the chicken coop before he exited and began to make his way inside. As he approached, the garage door began to open. It was less than three feet off the ground when Duke came charging out, wagging his tail.

Close behind was Brooke, looking more than a little upset.

"Where did you go?" she demanded.

Dale moved past her. "I went to take care of something."

"You went to get yourself killed is more like it."

He planted his feet and turned. "I did what I had to do."

"And what would I have done if you'd been killed?" Brooke said, rubbing her eyes to keep the tears away. "You don't have the right to take those kinds of risks. You're the only family I have left."

"Don't let Colton hear you say that," Dale said, regretting the comment the minute it came out of his mouth. He paused. "I'm sorry, Brooke. I don't know what to tell you other than seeing Shane the way he was, it just made something in me snap."

"Dad, you're trying so hard to do the right thing," she said, her arms folded over the Arizona State University shirt she was wearing. "But you don't seem to get it."

Dale shook his head. "What don't I get?"

"There is no right or wrong anymore."

Now it was Dale's turn to be upset. "I don't believe that, Brooke." He passed through the garage. The sun was mostly gone, throwing long shadows at their feet. "I refuse to believe that. We're not the bad guys here, Brooke. Sometimes good people have to do horrible things." Those inside the house began to enter the garage, drawn by the commotion. "I went to kill the source of our troubles today. The two men who were responsible for Shane's death."

"What happened?" It was Sandy who asked the question. Colton, Zach, Ann and Nicole stood nearby.

"Looks like you made it back in one piece," Zach said, grinning. "Wish I could say the same for the pickup."

Weapon in hand, Colton moved past them to peer around the corner of the garage and watch for threats from the street.

"It was a tight squeeze," Dale told him. "But nothing a buffer and a coat of paint can't fix." The brief smile that had formed on his lips quickly faded when he saw Zach's hand on Sandy's shoulder. Sandy nudged it off. But Dale's blood pressure was already rising. The ex-con was getting comfortable, maybe too comfortable.

Trying to stay focused, Dale clapped the chalky desert dust off his hands and proceeded to tell them everything that had happened.

When he was done, the shocked expressions on their faces spoke volumes.

"Are you sure Reid is dead?" Ann asked.

"I'd say so," Dale confirmed. "Unless he can take a fifty-caliber round to the brain and keep going."

Colton turned. "But that's a good thing, isn't it?" he said without much force, as though he were asking a dumb question and expected everyone to come down hard on him.

"It's either a very good thing," Sandy said, "or a very bad one."

"Why would Ortega do such a thing?" Nicole asked. Her eyes were puffy and red from crying. There was a heavy thread of fear in her voice. She seemed more than sad. She seemed nervous and agitated.

Zach cleared his throat. "I'll bet Ortega was still sore from the butt-whooping we gave him and the mayor went shooting his mouth off."

"That may be so," Dale admitted. "Though I'm starting to think something else was behind the mayor's murder. The cartel is cruel and unpredictable, that much we know. But they also came here with a plan and I think we just witnessed the first stage."

"They wanna take over the town," Sandy said, her hazel eyes deep with worry.

Dale shook his head. "They already have."

Chapter 9

The following morning they buried Shane's body under a tree next to the firing range. When Dale finally found the time he would clear out a larger section of brush to make room for additional gravestones. It was a depressing thought, but at some point each of them would pass one way or another and when that happened it would be nice if they had a dedicated cemetery. If they made it that far, he might even bring Julie and Lori's bodies back to the property for reburial.

Each of them took a moment to say a few words, Brooke and Nicole reciting mournful prayers. Dale told them a story instead, about how as a kid, whenever Shane would get punished by Ma or Pa, he'd pack his tiny suitcase with nothing but t-shirts and threaten to move out. They all had a much-needed laugh at that. When it was Colton's turn to speak, Dale noticed Zach leaning over more than once to whisper something into Sandy's ear. He watched her expression to see if she was annoyed or whether she was enjoying the attention Zach was giving her.

Zach and Dale couldn't be further apart. Which was why it was hard for Dale to believe that she could like both of them at the same time.

Slowly, he put any thoughts of jealousy out of his mind and drew his attention back to the hushed voices and those assembled. Perhaps the only real difference between this funeral and the others Dale had been to was that everybody here was armed. Surely the cartel knew by now that he had been the one to fire upon them from the knoll near the television plant. If so, both sides would more than likely be looking for vengeance. With Sheriff Gaines, that was normally accomplished in a fairly predictable fashion. Action and reaction. Which made anticipating a counter-attack little more than a simple calculation. But the cartel operated differently. They had assaulted Dale's fortress head-on in the beginning, but he knew that the next attack would come at the time and in the manner he least expected.

Listening to the others offering their final respects, Dale couldn't help wondering about Reid's execution the day before. If he'd felt before that Sheriff Gaines and Ortega couldn't be reasoned with, he knew it now without a single shred of doubt. How did you negotiate with men who were willing to leave you face down in the dirt in order to take what you had? He had contemplated this very question over the last few days and weeks when the violence between the two groups had begun to escalate. Like many of the conflicts around the world in the days before the virus had thinned the global population, the current crisis had no clear end in sight. They would either learn to coexist or destroy one another.

Historically, victory often went to the side with the greatest resources. That meant that Dale and those under his care were at a distinct disadvantage. If more of the cartel came to town or the townspeople were somehow turned against Dale's cause, it would only be a question of time before they were overwhelmed. A delicate game of diplomacy was underway, one Dale would have to play if they wanted any chance of surviving the weeks and months ahead.

With the ceremony done, they began heading back toward the house in twos and threes. Nicole was the last to leave and Dale stayed by her side until she was ready to go.

When they were alone, she no longer felt the need to hold back. "I blame you for what happened," she told him. "Your brother loved you, looked up to you and for that you got him killed."

Her words felt like hot stinging needles buried deep in his flesh. "I expected you to feel that way," he told her. "You loved him very much and you're grieving and I guess part of that means you're gonna look for someone to blame. I never asked for you and your family to come here. Don't get me wrong, I'll be forever grateful for everything you've done for us. But the four of you came of your own free will."

She regarded him from the corner of her eye. "All you had to do was give them what they wanted and Shane would still be alive. Because of that I'm not sure I'll ever be able to forgive you."

"I won't deny I've made mistakes," Dale said quietly. "There's no rulebook for how to act in a situation like this. All I can do is listen to my conscience and pray that I'm doing right by me and everyone else under my care. Sometimes that means making tough decisions. Sometimes that means people die, people we love, so that others may live. I won't pretend that I can make those decisions better than everyone else, but so far the responsibility has fallen squarely on my shoulders. If you and your parents wish to leave, I won't stop you. I'll be saddened, but I won't stand in your way."

50

Nicole shook her head and Dale wasn't sure if she was telling him she wanted to stay or whether leaving under the current circumstances was no longer an option.

For a moment, he considered pressing her on the subject but thought best to just let it go. Instead, he assured her he wouldn't stop until Shane's killers were made to pay, whether that meant at the end of barrel or at the end of a noose. The promise seemed to get through to her because Nicole took his hand, mouthing the words, "Thank you."

By the time they made it back to the house, Dale saw that Dannyboy was back on his feet, mingling with the others by the pumphouse. They were looking at something on the structure itself and talking excitedly amongst themselves.

He arrived and saw that somebody had spray-painted a symbol of some kind onto his pumphouse door. A circle wrapped around the letter V.

"This wasn't here when we came out earlier," Sandy said, puzzled.

The house had been locked up while they were out back but Dale decided to make a sweep of the property anyway to be sure whoever had done this wasn't still lurking around. After they were done, each of them returned to the pumphouse.

Dale ran his fingers over the red spray paint and saw that some of it came off on his fingers. "Sandy's right. This is still fresh. Whoever this was, they must've done it while we were burying Shane." He checked the door and found that it hadn't been tampered with. Dale couldn't tell what he found more unsettling, the fact that someone had so brazenly trespassed on his land or that the meaning behind the mysterious symbol had yet to be deciphered.

"You think it's a threat?" Brooke wondered aloud.

51

"Looks like one to me," Zach said, gripping his pistol. "A tag on the pumphouse. You don't need to be a whiz to figure out they're laying claim to what's ours."

"They wouldn't be the first," Dale said, trying to sound calm. "The real question is who are the ones laying the claim and why don't they come right out and ask for it man to man?"

Just then a figure appeared at the end of the driveway. Duke let out a series of vicious barks before Dale gave the order to heel and leveled his shotgun.

The figure approached, dragging a small cart behind him. Duke continued growling as the man approached.

"Is that pooch of yours ever gonna cut me some slack?" Billy asked, annoyed and maybe a little hurt. He glanced around and whistled when he saw the bodies stacked in front of the house. "I heard the shooting yesterday and wasn't sure whether you folks were still alive or not. Gave you fifty-fifty odds."

"How generous of you," Dale said.

Billy smiled. "Glad to see I was wrong."

"We still have a lot of cleaning up to do," Sandy explained, straining a smile. "If you're offering to help, we'll gladly accept."

Billy bent over laughing. "Wish I could, but I got a place of my own that's in desperate need of attention." His gaze drifted past Sandy's shoulder toward the pumphouse. "And I see I'm not the only one." He was talking about the graffiti.

Dale furrowed his brow. "You get one too?"

"Unfortunately, yes," Billy spat.

"You know who did this, old man?" Zach asked.

Billy fixed him with a penetrating glare. "Don't think I know this one."

"It's my father," Colton said proudly. Zach ruffled his son's hair and rested his hand on the back of his neck.

"Oh, I remember now. You're the felon."

Zach's features darkened. "That was a long time ago."

Billy let out the kind of laugh which made it clear he wasn't afraid of causing offense. "If you say so. Far as I'm concerned, anyone who survived the scourge has earned a clean slate. CEOs and street cleaners are equals now. It's what you do with the rest of the time you've been given. That's what matters most."

Zach eyed the rest of the group. "Maybe the old man's not as crazy as he looks."

That made Billy chuckle, until his gaze settled over that symbol again. "The folks who left that are nothing but a bunch of looters and vandals."

"You know them?" Dale asked, curious why Billy knew them and he was still in the dark.

"Not directly, no. But I heard about 'em. See, a man in my profession learns to keep his ear to the ground and his lips sealed tight. Word on the street is they started as a small group stealing non-perishables from abandoned houses. Before long they'd graduated to snatching whatever they could get their hands on. And now it seems they've found us, except I don't have nearly as much worth stealing as you do." Billy was pointing a grease-stained finger at Dale. "I'd watch out for them if I were you."

Billy's warning didn't sit well with Dale. Even after disposing of the dead cartel members and getting back to work on the removable staircase, Dale was still feeling concerned. The last thing they needed was another group coveting their resources. He was beginning to see now that his strategy of cutting himself off from the rest of the town was coming back to haunt him. More and more, Dale realized he needed to adapt once again to an ever-changing landscape or risk being isolated and destroyed. He needed allies and fast.

53

Chapter 10

Not long after, Dale called everyone inside. The garage had become something of a congregation zone in recent days, mostly since it faced away from the road and thus offered a level of concealment from attack. But the bushes and trees beyond the edges of the property left it somewhat vulnerable and so Dale had opted to hold the meeting up in his bedroom. That way they could all be present while also keeping an eye out for intruders. There was a lot to do and, as usual, too few hours in which to do it.

When everyone was assembled, Dale cleared his throat and began to speak.

"I remember Walter once told me that the difference between a successful mission and a failure was the debrief that took place between engagements." Looking around, Dale could see most of what he'd just said had sailed right over people's heads. "What I'm trying to say is that it's important to figure out what went wrong and how to make sure it doesn't happen next time. But before that, we should be congratulating ourselves for repelling Ortega's attack."

Not surprisingly, Nicole's eyes began filling with tears and she excused herself from the room. Ann went to follow her, but Dale asked her to stay. "She's not alone in losing someone she loved. She'll be fine, we need to just give her some space." He turned to Zach, Colton, Sandy and Brooke. "But I didn't call this meeting so we could pat each other on the back. What happened yesterday wasn't a sure thing. For a while it was touch-and-go and we need to lay out what lessons we learned and how to better prepare for the next attack."

"We need more ARs," Zach said. "I mean, at least one for everyone as well as some night-vision gear in case we get attacked after sundown."

Dale nodded. "We could definitely beef up our firepower, no doubt about it. I'll look into the night-vision."

"I also think we need to stash weapons around the house," Zach went on. "If those bastards manage to break down another wall, I don't wanna be caught on the john with nothing to defend myself."

Colton chuckled, covering his mouth as he tried to hold it in. Whenever the conversation offered Zach an opportunity to toss in some toilet humor, he was always quick to oblige.

"Zach on the toilet," Sandy said, shaking her head. "I'm sure the stench alone would send the cartel running."

The group let out a collective laugh. Much to everyone's surprise, Ann joined in, pitching in with a joke about a priest, a bishop and a monk who walked into a bar and asked to use the restroom. The joke itself wasn't one bit funny, but watching prim and demure Ann let her proverbial hair down had them all in stitches.

Dale felt the muscles in his stomach burning. But more than that, he felt the growing tension rolling off of him in the way that only the best of belly laughs could accomplish. Slowly the room settled, Dale reminding them how important the current conversation was.

"Well, the cartel attacked us with small arms," Sandy said. "But next time we might not be so lucky."

"Sandy's right," Colton said. "I remember seeing a show on Mexican drug lords and some of them had fifty-caliber Ma Deuces mounted onto Hummers."

"Just one of those would be enough to turn this place into a block of Swiss cheese," Zach said, looking around at the myriad of bullet holes already punctuating the room.

Lucky for them, Arizona featured an incredibly arid climate. If they were somewhere else, like Washington State where it rained at the drop of a hat, mold and mildew might be a real problem. At least there they weren't killing each other over water, Dale thought. Other things perhaps, but not water.

"Something else I noticed," Colton added. "We need to go through all those rounds and sort them by caliber. Once our initial magazines ran empty, it was taking forever to dig through the 9mm and 30-06s to get to the .223s."

Dale was writing all this down. "Since no one's stated the obvious," he said, "I'll be the one to put it out there. We need to find a way to stop bad guys from crashing vehicles into the house. Up until then, I'd say we were doing just fine."

"Sounds great, but how do you propose we protect against that?" Brooke asked. "I guess we could put concrete pillars across the front lawn."

"Sure, and I could paint them to look like garden gnomes," Ann offered.

Dale grinned. "I think the only viable option is to dig a trench. Doesn't have to be very deep or very wide. If the dimensions are laid out right, it'll be more than enough to stop a speeding truck. I'll crunch some numbers and see what I can come up with. But more pressing are the stairs Walter and Colton were working on right before this happened. Those need to be attached and made operational as soon as possible."

Dannyboy stepped forward, his head still covered in bandages. "The fancy defensive stuff y'all are talking about is great, but what's the point if one guy with a spray can is able to walk right up when no one's looking?"

"What about an automatic sentry gun?" Colton said sarcastically.

"I'm not kidding," Dannyboy said, annoyed. "Tech it up all you want. Dig a hundred ditches while you're at it. But it's human oversight that leads to most failures. Some folks call it user error. Let me be as clear as I can. Banks, back when they still existed, used to invest billions in anti-hacking firewalls and protective measures, and yet getting around their security was often as easy as leaving an infected thumb drive with the bank's logo lying around for some poor employee to find. The minute he plugged it into his computer, bam, he'd infected the entire network. Humans are the soft entry point. All I'm saying is let's make sure the same thing doesn't happen to us."

Dale was impressed and the look on his face must have showed it. "So how many banks have you hacked?" he asked Dannyboy, only half serious.

The skinny thief held up a hand. "I plead the fifth."

"It's an excellent point," Dale went on. "All of us were so caught up with grieving Shane's death that we didn't think to maintain security during his burial."

"Maybe we need more people to join us," Brooke said. "You know, open up diplomatic relations."

Dale looked at her and nodded. He'd been thinking the same thing.

The meeting finished soon after and everyone left to begin the work assigned to them. Dannyboy and Colton would finish the stairs, while Ann and Sandy would tend to the garden and the livestock. Every few hours, Ann would check in on Walter and change his bandages. As for Brooke, she had won the enviable task of sorting through the ammunition. Meanwhile, Sandy would join Dale out front to begin work on the ditch. Originally, he'd asked Zach to help him, but his brother-in-law told him he was going to take the pickup left by the cartel and see if he could find weapons, ammo or anything else of use. Colton's immediate impulse had been to go with his father and it had taken some serious cajoling to convince him to stay and finish his work.

Dale asked Sandy, his ditch-digging partner, to stay behind.

"That seemed to go well," she said with a touch of irony. She was referring to Zach, of course, and his reluctance to fall in line and fully join the group.

"He's always had a difficult time with authority," Dale said, hoping it didn't sound like he was making excuses. "It's been helpful having him around, even if sometimes I wanna pummel him."

Sandy raised her eyebrows. "That bad, huh? What'd he do to ruffle Mr. Hardy's feathers?" She whisked imaginary dirt off his shoulder as she used to do back when they were dating.

Dale debated whether he should say anything.

"Out with it," Sandy ordered. "Don't you think I know when you're hiding something?"

"He's been getting a little too touchy-feely for my taste."

Sandy's eyebrows arched. "With you?"

"No, not with me," he corrected her. "With you."

She grew silent, seeming to replay in her head each of the interactions she'd had with Zach. "He has been friendly, but I wouldn't categorize it as inappropriate."

Dale frowned. "I knew I shouldn't have said anything." He started to walk away.

"Dale Hardy, are you jealous?"

He glanced back. "What gives you that idea?"

"You are, aren't you?" Sandy began to giggle. "Men are so territorial sometimes."

The comment made Dale smile. Maybe she was right. This was his house and perhaps he'd blown things out of proportion. "Just promise you'll let me know if he steps out of line."

"If Zach crosses any lines," Sandy said, "then I'll fix him myself, thank you very much."

Standing in a beam of soft light, she looked even more beautiful. Unable to help himself, Dale crossed the distance between them in two short strides and pulled her in for a long kiss. He felt Sandy go limp in his arms before at last he pulled away.

A radiant smile filled her face. "What took you so long?"

Chapter 11
Sheriff Randy Gaines

The morning had begun for Randy with the stark realization that life in Encendido would never be the same. For some time, he lay on his cot replaying the seconds before Mayor Reid's head was made to look like a dead animal along the side of the highway. That was to say, red and covered in hair, but otherwise unrecognizable.

Ever since Dale's attack against the sheriff's office, Randy had ordered that the lunch room at the rear be converted into a temporary barracks. Out went the tables, chairs and the now empty vending machines and in came the army-style cots. There were fifteen of them in total, although currently only eleven were being used. The process of recruiting more deputies was becoming something of an uphill battle, especially after the arrival of Edwardo Ortega and his men. Surely, things would only grow harder once word of the Mayor's death began to spread.

The cartel's attack against Fortress Hardy, as some of the folks in town had taken to calling it, had proven to be a total and complete failure. A third of Ortega's men were either dead or wounded. Before charging off, Edwardo had assured them his men were more than up for the job. He'd even spat when Mayor Reid had suggested the deputies tag along as a reserve force in case he should need them. In hindsight, seeing that look of anger on Edwardo's face, his nostrils flared, his bloodshot eyes looking like roadmaps, it was clear Mayor Reid had just swung and missed. Strike one. The final strike would come after Edwardo and his men limped back, swearing incessantly in Spanish and firing their guns into the air in frustration.

It was no surprise that Ortega had blamed the mayor for the failure, telling him if his deputies were man enough to be there, they would have slaughtered the defenders and carried the day. It didn't matter that the mayor had told him to limit the bloodshed, that a surrender was preferable to an extermination. The mayor had given his word and he had intended to keep it.

Keith entered the barracks just then carrying a handwritten note. A few of the other deputies around him were stretching the kinks out of their backs from a bad night's sleep. Randy stood, rubbed his eyes and took the note from Keith. It was from Edwardo and in broken English instructed Randy to assemble his deputies out front in five minutes.

He glanced up at Keith, who looked just as surprised. "There's a small crowd gathered. Seems Edwardo's gone around and collected a bunch of the townspeople."

"Who gave you this note?"

"One of his enforcers," Keith said. "Big arms. Scar across his neck. Bandage on his right wrist."

"El Ventrílocuo," Randy muttered. "He say what this was about?"

"Contrary to his name, this guy doesn't say much."

61

"All right then," Randy said, his heart hammering in his chest as he wondered if he was about to witness another execution, perhaps this time his own. "I guess we do what the man says. How bad can it be, right?"

A look of deep concern flashed over Keith's face. For a moment he looked like he wanted to say something, likely something bad about Edwardo, but thought better of it. Had they already come to the point where even law enforcement had to bite their tongue for fear of being killed? Last Randy checked, they were the ones calling the shots, spreading fear through the population, taking whatever they pleased. Now the tables had turned and with them, so too had the contents of his stomach.

Minutes later, Randy and his ten deputies stood on the steps of the Sheriff's office. He'd arranged his men into two equal lines. Facing them was Edwardo Ortega and the remnants of his cartel enforcers—at least twenty of them, many bandaged and looking like they'd been through the washing machine spin cycle on high. Behind them were over a hundred Encendido citizens, many with deep looks of concern. Those dour expressions were countered by the grin on Edwardo's face. Whatever was about to happen right now, the drug lieutenant felt it was a reason to celebrate. Randy fought down that churning feeling in the pit of his belly, forcing a smile at the man who had killed his boss and was clearly up to no good.

Edwardo came forward, flanked by the cherubic El Grande and a rather sour-looking El Ventrílocuo. The rest of his men stayed where they were, carrying high-caliber automatic weapons. With their sun-baked skin covered in tattoos, they made a terrifying sight.

The cartel lieutenant held out his hand to Randy, who hesitated.

"Don't worry," Edwardo said. "I won't bite."

His men broke into rowdy laughter.

The two men shook.

Edwardo turned back to the crowd. "The people of Encendido have experienced untold suffering and tragedy over the past few months. It seems that God blinked and the world changed." Edwardo made the sign of the cross. "I've brought you all here to assure you that we care about your troubles. We were called in by the late Mayor Reid to provide security and safety for your town and we intend to fulfill that pledge. But security requires unity and above all loyalty." Edwardo turned back and raised one of Randy's hands in the air. "Sheriff Gaines, do you and your men swear to keep the people of Encendido safe?"

Randy felt the muscles in his neck stiffen. He watched his arm propped above his head. "We do."

"And do you swear to follow my leadership and all of my commands in the pursuit of restoring order and peace in Encendido?"

Seconds went by and Randy still hadn't responded. Some of the other deputies were looking around, perhaps unclear about what was happening.

Edwardo repeated the question and this time the tone of his voice left no doubt there was only one acceptable answer.

The tension among those in the crowd below was nearly palpable. Randy had sensed the shift in power the minute the cartel had walked through the front door of Reid's mansion. But never in his wildest dreams had he expected to be standing on the front steps of the sheriff's office, swearing an oath of allegiance to a criminal organization.

Randy swallowed hard, his throat as dry as a desert bone. "We do," he replied, his voice cracking.

"Louder," Edwardo ordered.

"We do." He complied, shouting the words as if he wanted nothing more than to fling them as far away as he could.

"That wasn't so hard, was it?" Edwardo said, his dead brown eyes twinkling in the summer heat.

He shifted and began shaking hands with each of the deputies. The cartel whooped and hollered while the crowd looked on, stunned, some of them confused, wondering what they'd just witnessed.

With bile crawling up his throat, Randy too was left to wonder whether future generations would study this moment, working out the exact second when Encendido had left the United States and become part of a dictatorship under the cartel's iron rule.

Chapter 12

After the stunned crowd began to melt away, Edwardo circled back to Randy, an expression of triumph on his face. The sight was certainly a radical departure from the rage Edwardo had exhibited after his defeat at the hands of Dale and his followers.

"I intend to succeed," Edwardo told him, "precisely where you and the mayor failed."

Randy watched most of his deputies shuffle back into the sheriff's office. "I don't think I follow you."

"Food, water and shelter," the cartel lieutenant told him. "Those are the basic ingredients of life. Whenever any one of those is absent, the population grows restless, even rebellious. Our first order of business is to increase food collection. We'll search houses that haven't been cleared, and place a goods tax on anyone growing their own produce. Use your imagination. We'll use the television plant to store what we gather. It's my job now to see to it that no one starves."

If Edwardo couldn't gain the people's loyalty with respect, he was equally capable of buying it with bribes.

"It's what you call the carrot and the stick," he said, seeming to read Randy's thoughts.

"Finding canned food and taking a farmer's crops is one thing," the sheriff said. "But out here, finding water is a different beast entirely."

Ortega patted Randy's chest playfully, the way a father might do to a child. "The water, you leave that to me."

"What about Dale Hardy?" Randy asked and the shift in Edwardo's expression was immediate. "We've got inside information now. I don't see why we wouldn't—"

"We need to be careful," Edwardo said, "to make sure we don't ruin the advantage we now possess."

"The note Dale sent us," Randy said. "It sounds like he's ready to negotiate."

"By the time I'm done with that man," Edwardo assured him, "he'll be begging us to take his water. Now have your men provide security for the food collection teams I've assembled."

Edwardo patted him on the back, like the two of them were great friends. Ortega had been right, securing the people's love and admiration was important. Just as important was burying anything that might cast you in a bad light. Randy would do as Edwardo ordered, but there was something he needed to do first.

•••

The Encendido health clinic was dark when Randy arrived. He pushed open the double doors and discovered a waiting room which had been turned into a full-blown convalescent ward. Over and above the regular townspeople, cartel members were being attended to by a small handful of nurses who moved

66

from patient to patient. He'd never seen the clinic this full.

A nurse named Natalie Krueger hurried past him. Blonde and over six foot tall, she had been dubbed 'the Amazon' on account of the way she towered over most other women, and even some men.

"I'm looking for Betty," he said when he finally caught up to her. What he didn't tell her was the reason why finding her was so important. The aging head nurse knew what Randy had done to Sheriff Joe Wilcox and a handful of others in a power grab Randy and Hugh Reid had orchestrated. If order was ever restored, Randy would be the only one to take the fall.

"She's not here, Sheriff," Natalie said, preoccupied. "As you can see I'm low on nurses and high on patients." She sounded annoyed. Randy figured most of her distaste came from caring for the drug lord's underlings, especially after they'd been wounded attacking fellow Encendido citizens.

"Any idea where she is?"

Natalie stopped what she was doing and looked at him. She had about two inches on Randy, which meant she was literally looking down on him, something his ego was having trouble with. "Betty left the clinic two days ago and I haven't seen her since."

That was around the time Randy had considered making Betty disappear, the way the others had disappeared. But somehow, the thought of Encendido losing a valuable member of the medical profession had stayed his hand. Thinking back, he saw he'd made the wrong decision.

Randy was about to leave when Natalie said something else, almost in passing.

"She left with two men. I assumed they were two of yours, come to escort her home. Nowadays one can never be too careful."

"Two men?"

Natalie appeared worried, as though she'd said something wrong.

"Had you seen them before?" he asked, wondering who they were.

"Never," she replied. "But the lighting in here isn't exactly top-notch. Speaking of that, I've submitted several requests to refuel the generator out back and haven't heard a thing."

"You're sure about the two men?" Randy asked again, ignoring everything else Natalie had said.

"Positive."

The problem, as far as Randy saw it, was that Betty didn't have any family left. So who would have come for her? Randy wasn't liking this one bit. "Where's Betty's office?"

Natalie sighed. "I'm really rather busy."

"This is important," he said, maybe a little too forcefully. Some of the other nurses around him stopped what they were doing and stared. "Go back to work, will you?" Reluctantly, they returned to their patients. "I need access to Dr. Peterson's office as well."

He could tell Natalie was thinking about how many laws Randy was in the process of breaking, a relic of the old days where the rule of law still meant something. But this new world had rules too. Eat or be eaten. And Randy had no interest in being someone else's lunch.

He spent the next several minutes searching both offices and coming up empty. If Dr. Peterson's medical reports on the men and women Randy had taken care of weren't here, it meant Betty must have taken them with her. He remembered finding Sandy and Betty speaking over the shortwave. Could his former deputy have something to do with this? Maybe, maybe not. But one thing was certain: the old nurse had the goods on Randy and he'd failed to come down hard when he had the chance. He wouldn't make the same mistake twice. He needed to find the identity of those two men and, more importantly, where they had taken her.

Chapter 13
Sandy

Sandy started the pickup and was about to leave the property when Dale stopped her.

"Where are you going?" he asked.

She threw him a sharp look which made it clear she wasn't required to answer that question.

"I'm not being like that," he said defensively. "You know after what happened, the cartel will be looking for any chance to get even."

Sandy lifted the pistol off the seat next to her. "I've got backup. But if you must know, we need fertilizer. Back when I was running patrols, I remember finding the Keller farm abandoned. I figured they might have what we need."

"That's ten to fifteen miles away," Dale objected.

"Fifteen miles north of Encendido, which means it'll be safer. Listen, Dale, I got along just fine before I came to live here. You seem to forget I was once a sheriff's deputy."

A faint smile formed on his lips.

Brooke came through the garage toward them. "Hey, where you going?"

Sandy laughed. "Not you too."

"Lemme come."

"It's fine with me," Sandy said, looking at Dale, who didn't look happy.

"Dad, I've been cooped up for weeks," his daughter protested. She tapped the holster on her hip and the pistol inside it. "We'll be fine."

"Take this with you," Dale said, disappearing into the house and returning with Walter's AR-15 and a walkie-talkie.

Brooke rolled her eyes.

Sandy was just as exasperated. Some things never changed. Six months ago, Dale was after his daughter about wearing her seatbelt. Now he was making sure they had adequate firepower.

"Be back in an hour," Sandy assured him.

"If you see Zach while you're out there, tell him to get his butt back here."

Brooke shook her head. "I don't think that would go over very well with Uncle Zach."

Dale seemed to consider that before tapping the hood and wishing them a safe trip.

During the drive, the two women spoke. Brooke wanted to know about Sandy's time as a deputy and whether she missed it. The question wasn't easy to answer. Of course Sandy missed doing what she could to help maintain order in the community, but after the death of Sheriff Wilcox, all that had changed. Little by little, the role of the deputies had become helping to further Randy and Hugh's personal agendas. The loyalty she felt to the force and the folks she'd worked with was strong, but in the face of blatant corruption, even that had its limits.

The conversation soon turned to happier times, fond memories Brooke had about her mother. Julie had been a joker, something few people knew about the woman. Practical jokes were her specialty and she'd pulled them when Dale and Brooke least expected it. One time, in the tenth grade, Julie had packed her daughter a 'special' sandwich for lunch. Brooke seemed to be reliving the moment in disgust as she described biting into what she soon realized was a cow tongue sandwich. Not a word of a lie. A cow's tongue, between two pieces of bread. A friend sitting next to her had nearly fainted. The others screamed.

But eventually Brooke had gotten even. She wasn't nearly as creative as her mother, and therefore decided that the old saran wrap over the toilet bowl was as good a gag as any. It was only after she'd heard her father cursing from the bathroom upstairs that she realized how her joke had backfired.

Sandy and Brooke both broke into a chorus of laughter which continued in fits and starts for several minutes. Afterward, the muscles in Sandy's stomach ached from the memory.

They were having a fine time together. But what amazed Sandy most was that Brooke hadn't said a word about Sandy's past relationship with Dale, nor that those old feelings had started to rekindle. Perhaps it was because Brooke didn't need to ask. Maybe she could already tell. Maybe she recognized the past was the past and the future was the only thing worth worrying about.

Soon after, they reached the Keller farm and turned into the lane. Not long after the outbreak, Deputy Sandy had swung by to check up on the family, only to find that all four of them were dead—Frank Keller, his wife Diane and their young sons Derek and Paul. She'd donned a mask before going into the house that day, the floorboards creaking under her as she made the horrible discovery.

She'd found the parents lying next to each other in their bedroom. Fifteen-year-old Derek was in the bathroom, slumped over the toilet. His younger brother, Paul, ten, maybe eleven, was downstairs on the couch, his legs curled under him. You didn't need to be a CSI to know the youngest had been the last to die. The scene at the Keller house had stayed with her and probably would forever. But similar scenes had played out across the entire country, maybe even the entire world.

Rather than leaving the truck out front where others might see it, Sandy parked it behind the barn. They stepped out, the hot Arizona sun baking the skin on their arms and the tops of their heads, before reaching the relative cool of the barn. In one corner were bags of fertilizer.

"Let's start by loading these into the truck," Sandy said.

Once they had finished, the two women searched for anything else of use.

Brooke gasped.

On instinct, Sandy drew her pistol. "What is it?" she asked, scanning the area without finding any threats.

"I saw someone in the house," Brooke said, her face ashen white, in spite of the searing heat.

Skeletal fingers clambered up Sandy's spine. "Everyone in that house is dead," she told Brooke. Inside, she saw one of the curtains move. As a sheriff's deputy such a sight would have been reason to go investigate. Now, it was reason to get going.

They hurried back to the truck and were climbing inside when a male voice called out to them. He sounded friendly.

73

"Come on," Sandy said, sticking the keys in the ignition.

The voice called out again, this time asking for Brooke by name. Both of them froze, fearful and perplexed. Sandy started the truck. If this person behind the voice turned out to be a threat, at least they could make a break for it.

When Sandy backed up and straightened out, two males in their twenties came into view. Both were wearing desert camo pants and beige shirts. They removed the bandanas which hid their identities. Sandy and Brooke sat idling in the car, wondering where this was going. They had called Brooke by name and Sandy caught the faint air of recognition on the girl's face.

They raised their hands to show they weren't armed, although Sandy could see they were carrying pistols in leg holsters and rifles slung across their backs.

"Looks like they wanna talk," Sandy said, still wary.

Brooke's window was already down and she called out to them. "First put your weapons on the ground."

They looked at each other before complying.

"Don't you remember me?" the young man on the right asked. He had dirty blond hair and a tall, lean build. He looked like someone more at home on a surfboard than in the Arizona desert.

"Caleb?" Brooke said, uncertain. "He was a friend from high school who moved to Utah right before the eleventh grade," she told Sandy. Her gaze returned to her old acquaintance. "You still have your dimples."

He and his friend began to head over when Sandy ordered them to stay where they were.

"We're not the bad guys," Caleb assured them.

"I hope you'll understand if we decide for ourselves," Sandy replied.

Caleb nodded and introduced his friend. "This is Parker, but everyone calls him Parks."

"What were you doing inside that house?" Brooke asked, getting out of the truck before Sandy could stop her. Sandy then did the same, her hand ready to grab her pistol in case things turned ugly.

Caleb held a hand up to block the sun. "Same thing you were doing in that barn, I suppose. Looking for supplies or anything else of value."

"I didn't know you were in town."

"We moved back about a year ago," he explained. "Decided to stay with my parents while I saved up for school. Guess it was the right decision. I hear things are really bad in Tucson right now."

"You staying at your parents' place?"

Caleb shook his head. "They passed when the virus showed up. Might have been some of the first to go. Made me wonder why not me. Why I was spared."

"We could use an extra pair of hands around our place," Brooke said. "Maybe two if Parks is interested."

"At Fortress Hardy?" Caleb said, grinning. "Don't look so surprised. We know all about what you and your father have done. More than a few people in town think your dad's a hero. Maybe because to others, he's a villain."

"Fortress Hardy," Sandy said, amused. "Guess it makes sense. But who's the 'we' you were talking about? Are you part of a larger group?"

"We are," Caleb told her. "There are close to thirty of us, with new members joining every day or so."

Brooke's face squished up. "New members?"

Caleb straightened his shoulders. "We're part of a resistance movement, Brooke," he said. "Our leader, Nobel, decided to rise up when Sheriff Gaines' men started stealing people's properties. Now with the cartel in charge of Encendido, I expect our numbers will start to grow. Our symbol is the letter V surrounded by a circle. It represents victory through unity."

Sandy recalled the spray-painted image on Dale's pumphouse. "We've seen some of your artwork," she said. "You two might have been shot for sneaking onto our land."

Caleb shook his head. "That wasn't us."

"Maybe not, but no one back at what you're calling Fortress Hardy appreciated you trying to lay claim to our water supply."

"That wasn't why they left it," Parks said, his voice that of a boy in his late teens. "It was meant to tell you one of our agents was reaching out. Consider it a calling card."

"Something tells me we aren't meeting by chance," Sandy said. "Is that what this was meant to be? The follow-up?"

Caleb nodded. "Let's just say we share the same goals."

"Don't be so sure about that," Sandy said curtly. "We just want to be left alone." She saw that Brooke was ready to object, but a subtle squeeze to the arm was enough to silence her. Caleb noticed the move.

"I know what you're thinking," Caleb said.

Sandy's left hand was on her hip. "Oh, do you?"

"You're thinking that sooner or later, we'll be no better than the cartel."

"That's how things tend to play out. At the beginning you stand for something honorable, but inch by inch circumstances force you to ignore your idealistic roots in order to deal with the real world. It's a slippery slope and you wouldn't be the first to take a slide."

Caleb's blue-eyed gaze settled on Brooke. "If you folks only want to be left alone, we'll respect that."

"I hope so," Sandy said, getting back into the truck. She leaned her head out the window. "Brooke, let's go."

A few seconds later, they drove past the two young men, Brooke watching from the window as they pulled away. The rest of the drive home was quiet. Sandy was intrigued to learn that a resistance movement had taken root in Encendido, although not entirely surprised. Caleb and Parks had mentioned they were led by someone who called himself Nobel—a name perhaps borrowed from Alfred Nobel, the inventor of dynamite and founder of the famed peace prize. Whatever its source, something told Sandy she'd be hearing the name more and more in the coming days.

Chapter 14
Nobel

Vickie Meeks, who went by the code name Nobel, stared up at Encendido Community College (ECC)—a handsome late-nineteenth-century building with a red tile roof and a white cupola. She was admiring the place that close to thirty men, women and children under her care now called home. And home it would stay until the movement she had started succeeded in removing Encendido from the grasp of wicked men and returning it to its rightful custodian. The people.

If someone had told her two months ago she'd be living in the basement of the local college, bunking with over two dozen strangers and running a resistance movement, she would have assumed the person was barking mad. Not so long ago she had taught American history in some of these very classrooms. Those long hours spent preparing lessons and grading papers were little more than a memory now. Set against a world where every scrap of food, every sip of water was a small miracle, the memories felt distant and trivial. And yet she also knew that she needed to pass along the stories she herself had been taught. About the founding of the country and the two great wars which had forged over centuries with blood and strife what had been undone in mere weeks by a microscopic germ. She knew it was easy for folks seeking safety for their loved ones to let lofty ideals like freedom and the liberties afforded to them by the constitution fall by the wayside. Who cared about a piece of yellowing paper when your stomach ached for something to eat? And that was part of the challenge she faced. Overcoming it would start with regaining control of the town and reinstating honestly elected leadership. When bellies were full and the people's desperate thirst had been quenched, Vickie could begin the work of helping them remember what so many had died to protect.

When the virus had come to southern Arizona, the first to shut down had been the schools. The concern was they would become breeding grounds for the disease, vectors for rapid transit back to homes where it was feared the real devastation would begin. It was a fear that had proven meritless, since even with the schools closed, the virus had continued to spread, reaching out like the skeletal digits on the Grim Reaper's hands.

The truth was, few people had stockpiled the type of food and supplies needed to keep them isolated and thereby safe until the disease moved on. A trip to the grocery store, a chore that once elicited boredom, had become the stuff of nightmares. The killer was too small to see with the naked eye, too small to detect on infected hands, on clothing or in blood—but large enough to lay waste to entire communities.

Ironically, although the schools were the first to go quiet, when the human race eventually recovered, they would be the last to start up again. And that was something Vickie was counting on. The day Mayor Reid and Sheriff Gaines had declared they were taking control of the town, her instincts had told her something wasn't right. Reputations had a way of following a person around. The social order as we understood it might have collapsed, but the disintegration of law and order had done nothing to erase the history of corruption and deception both men shared. In a nutshell, Vickie had smelled a rat from day one, although finding the proof to back her allegations up... that had proven to be something else entirely.

The sudden appearance of the cartel had made her goals all the more pressing, all the more difficult. Distasteful as they were, at least Sheriff Gaines and Mayor Reid hid behind the tattered cloak of democracy. On the other hand, Edwardo Ortega and the hired thugs loyal to his father, the drug lord Fernando Ortega, cared nothing for pretense. Like the tribes that swept over ancient lands in the final days of the Roman Empire, they brought with them a violent autocracy that ruled by fear and intimidation.

Much to her surprise and dismay, Vickie's vision of a new Encendido was not shared by all. While she had been growing her movement one member at a time, a former bail bondsman named Calvin Pike had started a group of his own. Far from championing the cause of democracy, Calvin believed the town needed a strongman, but unlike Mayor Reid, one who believed in justice. No doubt he envisioned himself as that enlightened monarch who could lead the community and maybe someday the state back to normalcy. But as Vickie's teenaged son Thomas liked to say, his idea was good from far, but far from good. He was advocating a system with few if any checks and balances. Even if Calvin turned out to be a noble dictator, what guarantee was there that his successor wouldn't be a tyrant? These were the very concerns which had pushed a young America into the arms of democracy in the first place. With Calvin, the tragedy wasn't simply that the two groups hadn't been able to find common ground in order to work together. It was that Calvin believed bloodshed and the death of innocent civilians was inevitable, perhaps even required. Vickie saw things differently. She was certain she could destroy the current dictatorship from the inside out, the way the virus had destroyed their country. And that was why she'd reached out to someone close to Mayor Reid, someone who she felt represented a strong first step in finally liberating the town and starting fresh.

The irony of Vickie's less violent approach was that her husband, Bob Meeks, had been the proprietor of the town's largest gun shop. H3N3 had taken him early, in part because of the crowds that had flocked to the store in search of weapons to protect their belongings. Within the first couple of days, the shelves had been stripped bare, but that was mostly because Bob hadn't restocked them. He had decided to keep the bulk of the pistols and long guns—all in a variety of calibers—secured in the shop's basement. It was no surprise that before long the store had become target *numero uno* for local townspeople worried they'd be left defenseless when society collapsed completely.

She and Thomas had spent most of the night loading up an old box truck and carting countless crates to the college's sub-basement level. This stockpile, above all, was what Calvin and his followers wanted most. But he wasn't the only one. The Encendido authorities had also caught wind of a clandestine nighttime move and wanted her weapons—if not for them to use, at the very least to prevent them from being used against the sheriff and his men.

Contemplating Calvin's frightening vision of the town's future, Vickie couldn't help thinking about the items she'd seen on the nightly news before the televisions themselves finally shut off for good—the war in Syria and the disparate groups vying for control over that fragmented country. They were divided by religion and tribal alliances and in some cases by the same petty divisions that existed in Encendido. And it was their inability to unite against the dictator who ruled them that had ultimately led to their failure and eventual demise. She prayed the vying resistance factions in Encendido would not suffer the same fate.

Chapter 15

Dale

Another morning began with too little sleep. Dale swung his legs over the side of his bed and stretched his sore arms into the air. The space next to him in bed was empty, but he hoped it wouldn't remain that way forever.

He'd been relieved when Sandy and Brooke made it home safely yesterday bearing gifts. He had asked them about their trip, but neither had said much, which told him either it had been uneventful or there was something they weren't willing to divulge.

Soon after them, Zach had also returned, driving a dirty old Brinks truck, struggling to get the lumbering beast around the concrete pylons.

Dale had peppered him with questions, all of them well deserved. Where had he gotten the truck? What had he done with the pickup? Each of Zach's answers had been vague and unsatisfactory, other than to assure Dale they now had the equivalent of a tank. Dale's response had been to shake his head. A tank wasn't what they needed most. The two men seemed to have very different ideas on how to deal with the present situation, which left Dale to wonder how much longer they could continue before the friction between them ignited a fireball.

Following a quick breakfast, everyone armed themselves, as was their habit before work, and headed off to complete their given chores.

Dale had spent a few hours continuing the trench out front when he was approached by Sandy. The expression on her face was strange and right away Dale's heart began to gallop. Normally a look like that signaled bad news.

"What's wrong?"

All she could do was shake her head and cover her mouth, making it hard to tell if she was fighting back tears or laughter.

"You better see it for yourself."

He sighed, set the shovel down and followed her. As they rounded the front of the house, Zach's latest acquisition came into view, accompanied by the sound of splashing water.

Dale's jaw practically hit the ground when he saw Zach washing the grime off the Brinks truck. Ann and Brooke were there too, looking on disapprovingly.

"Are you out of your mind?" Dale shouted.

Zach stopped and regarded him strangely. "I know, she was a real mess, but I'll get her shiny and new, don't you worry."

"The only thing I'm worried about is how much water you're wasting." Dale watched the large puddle of soapy water gathered around the truck with disbelief. "I don't even have words for what you're doing, Zach. Don't you understand that people are dying of thirst?"

Zach let the sponge in his hand plop back into the bucket. "Who'd have guessed, the way you hoard every drop?"

The muscles in Dale's jaw tensed. "I don't need to explain myself to you. From now on, you don't get so much as a cup of water to brush your teeth unless you check with me first."

Zach didn't like that, not one bit. "We'll see about that." Colton stood by the pumphouse, watching the scene play out. Zach regarded his son and walked past him toward the firing range out back. Colton and Dannyboy followed him.

Still speechless, Dale stood glaring at the pool of wasted water.

"That could have been a lot worse," Sandy said, referring to Zach's notorious tendency to fly off the handle. "Look on the bright side. No one got shot."

"I won't tiptoe around someone with major impulse problems who lacks common sense."

"He stood by us when the cartel came knocking," Sandy reminded him. "That's gotta count for something."

Dale nodded. "Of course it does. But should that give him carte blanche to run through the limited resources we have? I don't want his help saving our lives if he intends to put them at risk by being foolish."

"You've also got Colton to think about," she said. Sandy had a knack for finding Dale's blind spot in any given situation.

"How so?"

"For better or worse, Zach is Colton's father."

Dale laughed sardonically and pointed a thumb over his shoulder. "When Zach was off doing time in Florence, I was the one picking Colton up from football practice. When Colton failed woodworking, I was the one who showed him how to fit a mortise and tenon joint."

Ann came over. "I believe Zach has never felt like he belonged anywhere before."

"Maybe that's for good reason," Dale said, quickly regretting the comment.

"I came from a small, rather dysfunctional family," Ann told them. "As a young girl, I fantasized about one day having a home bustling with little ones." Her old eyes grew red. "After I married Walter, we tried for years to have children but I guess the Lord decided against it. Maybe it was Walter's stubborn side, but he never gave up talking me into the idea of adopting."

"Nicole was adopted?" Sandy said, leaping ahead.

Ann nodded. "That's why Walter and I are so old. We nearly missed the window when a parent has the patience to deal with children and their shenanigans. Most of us aren't surprised when a teenager acts the fool. Kids will be kids, right? But sometimes when something very bad happens to someone, they can get stuck, emotionally." Her frail hand touched Dale's chest. "They look and sound like adults, but inside is just a scared little kid."

She was talking about Zach and Dale was about to respond when Ann glanced past him and shouted, "Jiminy Cricket, what on earth do you think you're doing?"

Dale and Sandy spun around to find Walter in the doorway to the house, his quivering hands gripping the frame as he struggled to stabilize himself.

They ran over to help him.

"I'm thrilled you're awake, but you shouldn't be out of bed," Ann scolded him.

Dale was far too thrilled the old man was still alive. "Maybe we should bring you back upstairs," Dale suggested.

"I came down for some fresh air," Walter said, having trouble speaking. They brought him out into the sun where he raised his head, like a plant, eager for nourishment. When his gaze returned to earth, it settled on the Brinks truck.

"I see you made a trade-in."

Dale laughed. "Trust me, you don't wanna know."

After a few moments of sunshine, Dale brought Walter back upstairs. Ann, Sandy and Nicole gathered at the foot of his bed, beaming with happiness.

"You thought I was a goner, didn't you?" Walter said, always cheeky.

"I won't lie," Dale admitted. "You aren't out of the woods yet."

"Men from my generation were built to last," he replied. "Not like the cheap plastic stuff nowadays that falls apart as soon as the warranty runs out."

Wounded or not, the old man hadn't lost his edge.

Walter looked at Ann. "Will you give me a minute with Dale?"

"Of course," she said. "Just don't go straining yourself."

He laughed. "She's one tough nurse, let me tell you."

The three women left and Walter grew serious. "I take it from the fact that you and I are still standing here that we won."

"We did, but the situation's become"—Dale paused—"more complicated."

"Were there any casualties?"

"Shane," Dale said, fighting back a surge of emotion and the impulse to explain any further.

"I'm sorry to hear that. Having Zach and his young friend Dannyboy probably made a real difference."

Dale reluctantly agreed. He didn't want to get into the troubles the two men were having. It was something they'd need to learn to sort out for themselves.

"This place has become something of a castle," Walter said. "But every good castle had one thing that we're missing."

"A moat?" Dale said. "Believe it or not, I'm working on that."

"No," Walter replied. "An escape tunnel."

The old man's answer caught him off guard. The thought had never crossed Dale's mind.

"If we're ever facing a hopeless situation, we need to find a way for some of us to get out safely. How better than right under the enemy's noses?"

"Where would it lead to?" Dale wondered aloud.

"The barn out back," Walter said without hesitation. "It's best to avoid coming out in the open and risk being seen. From there we could make our way past the firing range. The barn and the brush beyond would provide at least some concealment from enemy forces." Walter struggled for breath and Dale encouraged him to take it easy. "It'll take some doing, but I know you can do it. You never know when it'll come in handy."

Dale couldn't help but agree, although the thought of running from the property seemed so counter-intuitive. If push came to shove, where would they go? How would they live? The questions that arose from such a scenario were plenty and the answers few. Dale told Walter he should rest.

Most of the basement had been finished in concrete, apart from a crawlspace where the floor was mostly loose dirt. He headed downstairs to have a look and saw that a tunnel leading from the crawlspace to the barn was not only possible, it was vital. Walter had been right, it would be hard work, but one day it might just save their lives.

Chapter 16

Zach

"I still think he coulda done more to save his brother's life," Dannyboy was saying to Zach and Colton, who were out back by the firing range. Dannyboy was a few feet away, standing before Shane's grave.

"I'm sure his widow Nicole would agree with you," Zach said.

"Guess I just don't understand what was holding him back," Dannyboy went on. "I could kill a thousand cartel goons and never feel satisfied."

"That's because you're still sore over Hawkeye," Zach told him. "And I don't blame you one bit, brother. I had about twenty loyal bikers by my side and Ortega and his men cut most of them to shreds before they had a chance to fire a single shot."

"We could hear the battle from the house," Colton said. "That's why we jumped in the truck to come help."

Zach remembered how quickly Dale and the others had swung into action, even after he'd told them to stay back. At the time, he'd been sure his posse was about to teach those drug dealers a lesson. He still had a hard time accepting that he had been the one to get schooled that day.

"It was a good thing you listened. Y'all would have only gotten yourselves killed coming out in the open like that," Zach said. "They were waiting for us. It wasn't more than sheer luck that any of us got away. Maybe your uncle Dale doesn't get it, but I intend to have my revenge on those scumbags whether he's part of the plan or not."

Colton's eyes fell to Shane's grave. "I guess he can't help feel responsible for all the people living in the house."

"He's got a Superman complex," Dannyboy shouted. "I seen it before. Guys who take the weight of the world on their shoulders."

"Man's gotta take care of himself, first," Zach said in a low voice. "Don't you agree, Colton?"

Zach could see his son nodding, but the young man's eyes were saying something else.

"If we only ever look out for ourselves," Colton began, "what about the people who need help?"

"You know what I learned in prison?" Zach said. "Nobody cares whether you live or die. Not the people in the cell next to you, not the guards or the warden and especially not the people on the outside. You're the lowest of the low. Gangs form, don't get me wrong. But there isn't place in any of 'em for the weak."

"Do you think Ann is weak?" Colton asked, careful not to sound like he was challenging his father.

"That frail old lady?" Dannyboy said. "Hell, yeah."

Zach laughed. Dannyboy had a knack for saying more in a couple of words than most men could say in an hour.

"If she wasn't with us, who would grow our vegetables or take care of the chickens? Who would look after the wounded?"

"I don't know," Dannyboy said dismissively. "The same person who took care of that stuff before she was around."

"That was Dale," Colton answered. "But then he wouldn't be able to do anything else."

"What's your point?" Zach said, getting annoyed.

"All I'm trying to say is that everyone's got a place, even if they can't fire a gun real well or win a fistfight."

Dannyboy cackled with laughter. "Ann in a fistfight. Now there's a sight."

"Well, none of that changes the fact that the cartel keeps growing while we're stuck here watching Ann grow veggies. I'm guessing even you can see I'm right."

Colton nodded, somewhat reluctantly, but he did so nevertheless, even if it was to win his father's approval.

"We need reinforcements," Zach said. "We need to build a group of tough SOBs who won't shy away from giving those kingpins a taste of their own medicine."

Dannyboy perked up. "How do you figure on doing that?"

"I'm not sure, just yet," Zach said. "But I'm starting to think it may involve leaving this farm and striking out on my own."

"Not without me," Dannyboy said. "I wouldn't dare miss an opportunity to even the score."

"What about you?" Zach asked, eyeing his son. "We leave, will you join us?"

Colton's gaze flitted between them. He didn't say a word, but as far as Zach was concerned, he'd said more than enough.

•••

Dale

It was the middle of the night when Dale awoke, the soft squeal of the windmill churning outside his window mixed with the repetitive sound of Duke's light snoring from the foot of his bed. Otherwise, the house was quiet.

Faint threads of light bled in from the hallway, or was it the kitchen downstairs? Nearly everyone took turns on sentry duty and so it wasn't unheard of that some lights would be left on as the person in question made their rounds. Dale checked his watch. It was still Nicole's shift. He knew that because he'd nudged her awake before plopping into his own bed, dead tired after a long day of hard labor. The urge to close his eyes and drift back to sleep was strong and yet something about that light bothered him. Dale got out of bed and made it all the way to the door before backtracking to grab the .45 caliber Ruger he kept on the nightstand next to his pillow. By then Duke was on his feet, tail wagging.

He chambered a round in the pistol, but kept the safety on as the two of them made their way downstairs, Dale's bare feet whispering along the hardwood floor, Duke's nails clicking softly alongside him.

After a brief search, he couldn't find Nicole on the first or the second floor. And that sick feeling in the pit of his belly began to return. But was he overreacting? With the house locked down, there was no way for any of Ortega or Sheriff Gaines' men to sneak inside without Duke going absolutely haywire. Who needed an alarm system when you had Duke?

With that in mind, Dale made his way into the basement, certain there was a perfectly logical explanation. Maybe she'd decided to flout the rules and head into the basement to find something to eat. He wouldn't be happy, but that would be nothing compared to wasting precious water in order to wash a Brinks truck.

Dale was halfway down the stairs when he heard Nicole speaking.

"I tried," she said, weakly.

A male voice replied that she needed to try harder.

Drawing closer, Dale saw she was on the shortwave.

Nicole jumped and screamed with fright when she saw Dale standing a few feet away, his facial features twisted in puzzlement.

"Dale, you scared the heck out of me."

"What's going on here?"

"What do you mean?"

Dale's patience was wearing thin. "Who were you speaking with?"

There was a pregnant pause. "My uncle up in Scottsdale," she said at last. "I was just checking up on him."

"You're lying," Dale said.

"Excuse me?"

"Don't play the offended one with me," he snapped. "Unless you can talk to ghosts, that wasn't your uncle. Walter already told me everyone in your extended family is either dead or missing."

And in a horrible flash, Dale suddenly understood what was going on. She was talking to Sheriff Gaines, or at the very least to one of his men, revealing details about the defenses they'd erected and ways to overcome them.

The person on the other end of the radio could only hear you when you depressed the button and spoke into the mic, which meant whoever was on the other end was deaf to the conversation he was having with Nicole.

"Ask them something," Dale ordered her.

"What?" The tremble in her voice rose sharply. He could hear the way her tongue was sticking to her palate, a clear sign of dry mouth and an obvious indication of nervousness and guilt.

"I wanna hear their voice. You say it's your uncle, then I want you to ask him about the weather in Scottsdale." The gun was in Dale's hand. He wasn't prepared to use it, not just yet, but she didn't need to know that.

Nicole hesitated before doing as he asked. "How's the weather down there?" she asked, wincing.

"Weather?" The voice on the other end let out a distinctive-sounding laugh, one Dale had heard many times before. "What are you talking about, babe?"

And with that the blood drained from Dale's face and the strength went out of his legs. He knew who she'd been speaking with. Knew it wasn't Randy or one of his deputies.

The man on the other end wasn't her uncle from Scottsdale.

It was Shane.

Chapter 17

Dale woke everyone in the house by banging a pot with a metal spoon. The sound of cursing—nearly all of it emanating from Zach and Dannyboy—rolled down at him from the rooms upstairs. Sleepy-eyed and grumpy, they slowly assembled in the living room, the early-morning sky still a darkened mass.

"For the love of God, this better be important," Zach complained. "I was on a beach in Acapulco sipping Mai Tais and chatting with a redhead in a bikini."

Dannyboy chuckled, wiping the gunk from the corners of his lips.

"I was being chased by Mayor Reid's corpse," Sandy said, cupping her elbows and shivering.

"A shrink would have a field day with that one," Zach told her. His gaze then shifted over to Nicole, who was sitting in a chair facing the rest of them. "Someone's in trouble. Lemme guess, she used a bucket of water to flush a number one instead of letting it mellow."

Even Colton couldn't help but smirk at that one.

"Quit screwing around," Dale barked uncharacteristically, his thundering voice devoid of any humor. "I wouldn't have called you all out of bed if it wasn't serious."

He started to explain what had happened. By the time he arrived at the part where Shane was still alive, one side of the room was sitting in stunned silence while the other erupted into a volley of questions and comments.

"I mean, how's that even possible?" Colton asked, his hands at eye level as though he were trying to pluck something out of thin air.

Sandy shook her head in astonishment. "We buried him."

Their confusion was understandable. Dale himself was still trying to understand what had happened and, more importantly, why. Not surprisingly, Nicole wasn't saying much.

"So the two of 'em are working with Sheriff Gaines," Zach said with disgust.

"It appears so," Dale replied. "You can see now why this isn't the time for potty humor."

Ann was off to the side, weeping quietly. Nicole saw her mom and began crying herself.

"If Shane's still alive," Brooke began, choosing her words carefully, "then who did we bury?"

"Could be anyone," Colton said.

Dale wasn't so sure. "Not to get too graphic, but they needed to use someone recently dead."

"Also someone about the same height and weight as Shane," Sandy added. Her days as a deputy were no doubt kicking in.

"Then it sure as heck wasn't any of the bikers I rode in with," Zach assured them. "Those boys were grizzlies to a man." He stopped himself. "Unless it was Hawkeye. He was killed minutes before the cartel attacked us." His gaze shifted to Nicole. "What was the point of all this?"

She sat with her arms crossed, not saying a word.

"Give me ten minutes and I'll get her talking," Dannyboy said. Hawkeye had been his childhood friend and the thought of the cartel desecrating his corpse no doubt infuriated him.

Dale would never allow that to happen, but decided to remain quiet. If empty threats would get Nicole talking, he was more than happy to indulge Zach's young friend.

Dannyboy stood up and made a threatening move toward Nicole, who stuck out her arms to shield herself. "He wanted what was rightfully his," she said, spewing the words like they'd been trapped behind her lips for months, maybe even years.

Dale looked on in stunned amazement.

Her eyes met Dale's and she struggled to hold his intense glare. "He loved you, Dale. Believe it or not, he loved you to death. He wanted you to be proud of him. Seemed nothing he ever did was good enough. Same went for your father. When Dale got the property, I guess for Shane that was a final slap in the face."

"So he decided to have us killed and take it for himself," Dale shouted in disbelief.

Nicole shook her head. "He made an agreement with Mayor Reid that you, my parents and myself were not to be harmed. Once you were cast out, we would run the well on the mayor's behalf."

"And what about the rest of us?" Colton asked. Zach, Sandy and Dannyboy were just as eager to hear what she had to say.

She shook her head, her eyes downcast.

"We were as dead as dog meat," Zach said, then turned to Duke. "No offense, ol' boy."

Dale pivoted toward Ann, who was still crying, his voice soft, wounded, as he said, "Please tell me that you weren't part of this." Ann and Walter had become like parents to Dale and the thought of being betrayed by them was almost too much to bear.

"They had nothing to do with this," Nicole swore, seemingly relieved to be getting it out, but also visibly frightened with the looming prospect of punishment or even death.

"So that time Shane took off in the pickup," Dale began.

"He'd gone to meet with Sheriff Gaines," Nicole replied, hardly missing a beat. "To insist that he wouldn't help them unless he guaranteed your safety."

"Oh, how noble," Zach spat.

Brooke's eyes went wide. "And the goats? He poisoned them, didn't he?"

Nicole's eyes closed as though anticipating a blow. "No, that was me."

Colton just shook his head. "This keeps getting better and better. Next you're going to tell us one of you killed JFK."

Dale lifted his face, which had been buried in his hands. "So let me get this straight. We'd be turfed out to die and the two of you would carry on as if nothing had happened? Did you really think a principled man like your father would allow that?"

"We didn't think that far ahead, I guess."

"Of course you didn't," Dale went on. "But there's one thing that isn't adding up for me. Shane was far too lazy and frankly self-involved to conspire his way out a paper bag. Someone else had to be pulling the strings, putting ideas in his head, poisoning his mind even more."

Nicole hid her face in her hands and wept, rocking back and forth. But even Dale could see those weren't the tears of remorse. No, after the pain of Julie's passing, Dale knew what it meant to be gutted. The tears in

Nicole's eyes were the tears of regret. Regret at having been caught.

"The next order of business," Zach said, "should be finding a rope and a tree tall enough to hang her from."

Dale didn't say a word. Not because Zach was wrong, but because he was trying to decide how right he was.

Chapter 18
Randy

Dawn had turned to early morning when Edwardo Ortega and his group of bodyguards showed up at the sheriff's office. Many of the deputies who hadn't been working the night shift were only starting to stir.

Edwardo strode right into the barracks area, stuck the tips of both pinkies into his mouth and let out an ear-shattering blast.

"Good morning, my friends," he said in a rare display of joviality. "You know what they say. The early bird gets the worm." Which sounded to Randy's tired ear more like, "De hearly bur gets da whurm."

But it was the blaring truck horns drifting in from outside which really caught his attention.

"What's this all about?" Randy said, trying his best to hide his annoyance. A man thought twice about offending his boss when the man in charge was a cold-blooded killer. That the sheriff himself was also guilty of murder—and more than one—didn't seem to register in his sluggish early-morning brain. Either way, psychos and sociopaths always seemed to be the other guy.

Randy and his deputies dressed and shuffled outside. If this was another oath-taking ceremony, Randy wasn't sure what he'd do. Those horns blared again as three water trucks came roaring down the street, the cartel flag stenciled along the side. Gone were the days when the drug lords needed to hide from any government. Perhaps the reason was simple. In many cases they had simply taken the government's place.

The three trucks swung into the sheriff's office parking lot. A handful of townspeople whose houses were along Coronado Boulevard poked their heads out. Many even cheered. Randy shook his head in disbelief. It was a sight he would never have expected.

Edwardo and his bodyguard headed inside the office, followed by Randy and his deputies.

"When I give my word," the cartel lieutenant said with a toothy grin, "do I not deliver?"

"This will go far in helping the people of Encendido accept you," Randy said, trying to be positive.

Edwardo didn't like that. "Accept me? Why wouldn't they accept me?"

Randy's palms began to moisten. "I don't know, I'm just saying." This guy was acting like a Mexican Joe Pesci. Even the deputies around him looked nervous.

"Just saying? Your citizens are thirsty. I bring them water and you imply that we are not welcome here."

Keith cleared his throat. "Sheriff Randy's just saying that folks here were just getting used to Mayor Reid before his recent… departure. But we're all confident your generous gift will go a long way to help win them over."

The features on Edwardo's face softened. Then a smile appeared. He was happy again, at least for now. "Consider it the first of many more deliveries. Compliments of my father, Fernando. Not far behind these are trucks filled with food. One way to deal with men like Señor Dale is to cut them off at the knees. He thinks distributing water himself will win him friends. I intend to show him the error of that thinking."

Just then the front doors swung open and in walked a handful of Ortega's men. In the middle of the group was Shane Hardy.

"I take it you two know each other," Edwardo said.

"Where's Mayor Reid?" Shane asked, sounding more than a little nervous and looking like he hadn't slept in days. His right arm was bandaged, likely a wound he'd received during the battle over Dale's property.

Edwardo regarded Shane thoughtfully. "I'm afraid Mr. Reid is no longer with us."

Shane's eyes darted over to Randy. "We had an agreement."

"But you failed to live up to your end," Edwardo said. "You were supposed to get us that property and for that we would allow the safe passage of those inside. It was not our fault that your brother chose to ignore the 'kidnappers'' demands."

"Nicole was supposed to convince them if they had any doubts," Shane said. He spoke like a man pleading for his life, and maybe he was. "She told me she tried, but that Dale was worried about risking the lives of everyone else. The plan was to set up a meeting after they discovered the ransom note."

A vein in Edwardo's forehead began to throb with visible anger.

Randy shook his head. "Maybe Edwardo is right. Perhaps your brother was happy to see you go. The second he finds out what you've done, he'll have nothing in his heart but hatred for you. Mayor Reid said you were the ace up his sleeve, the one who would help rid us of Dale. You played your hand and like it or not, your brother called your bluff. As far as I'm concerned, you're useless to us now."

Edwardo seemed to agree. With a flick of his wrist, he ordered his men to take Shane away.

"We could keep him locked up here at the sheriff's office," Randy offered. "Until you decide what you wanna do with him."

"That sounds fine. But I'm not convinced yet he's as useless as you think," Edwardo said. "Do we still have his wife on the inside?"

Randy shrugged. "Hard to say. Shane did speak with her yesterday. Said she was acting a little funny, but didn't think their cover had been blown."

"Let's hope it stays that way."

Suddenly, an explosion from outside rocked the sheriff's office, blowing out windows along the eastern wall and sending ceiling tiles tumbling around them. Everyone ducked for cover, except for Edwardo, who spun on his heels and rushed through the front doors, his men rising and following briskly behind him.

Pistols drawn, Randy and his deputies did the same. His first thought was that they were under attack. Retaliation for the assault on Dale's place.

Smoke billowed from separate fires around the corner. They rushed in that direction, but Randy didn't need to see to know what was there. All three water trucks had been destroyed, each of their hulls torn open by a shaped charge of some kind. The metal on each bent inward, leaving a gaping hole where the water went rushing out, quenching the thirsty ground, most of it splashing into the nearby sewer drain.

There was a wooden fence that separated the parking lot from the row of houses beyond it and on that fence someone had used black paint to draw something. Looked like a circle with two intersecting lines. A set of crosshairs.

"I'll skin him and his entire family alive for this," Ortega barked furiously. He was talking about Dale, of course, but Randy wasn't so sure he was the culprit. During his attack on the sheriff's office, Dale hadn't left any kind of calling card. Didn't seem to be his style.

A crowd of townspeople had gathered to see what was going on.

"This may be someone else," Randy said.

"Grab one," Ortega told his men, pointing toward the group of people gawking at the destruction.

"What are you doing?" Randy asked, afraid of what Edwardo's temper might lead him to do.

Two of his enforcers approached the crowd, which started to scatter, but not before they grabbed hold of a thin man in his late twenties wearing a gray t-shirt. They dragged him over as he attempted in vain to resist.

"Symbols are important to you," Edwardo shouted, as though those who had blown up his trucks were listening. "Well, they are important to me too. So here's what will happen every time you destroy something of mine." He cocked the hammer back on his pistol and raised it to the man's head. Randy stepped forward to stop him, but he couldn't get there before the gun went off, killing the man. The cartel enforcers let his body flop to the floor like a child's doll.

Randy opened his mouth to say something as Edwardo blew a trail of smoke from the barrel of his gun. "You have something to say, Sheriff?"

"You didn't need to do that."

"Oh, but I did," Edwardo replied. "And if the people in this fine town don't start falling in line, there'll be a lot more where that came from."

Images from the old newsfeeds of ISIS killing large numbers of any who dared oppose them began to flash before Randy's eyes.

"Now do your job and find out who destroyed my water trucks. Because if you can't, then I will and you can bet I won't be nearly as nice."

Chapter 19
Dale

Watching Colton work the pulley system to lift and lower the retractable stairs was a sight to behold. They had offset it slightly from the middle back window so the opening could still be used as a firing position. More importantly, it meant that they now had more than one option for entering and exiting the house. Like the stone keeps from the Middle Ages, if a threat were to present itself, everyone could quickly enter the house and raise the stairs. Dale also had them include a failsafe in case the addition became stuck or otherwise inoperable. Two pins and key joints could be pulled and the stairs kicked off the metal hinge which held them in place.

"Not bad if I do say so myself," Colton shouted from the upstairs window.

"If I didn't know any better, I'd swear you were a master carpenter," Dale cried and gave him a thumbs up.

Standing next to her father, Brooke didn't look pleased.

"What is it, honey? I thought you'd be happier when the job was finally done." He wondered if the incident with Nicole was still weighing heavily on her. The whole situation still felt unreal, like watching a movie and somehow knowing in the back of your head that you were seeing scenes from your own life. They had locked Nicole in one of the bedrooms, her hands and feet bound, while they tried to figure out what to do next.

After the group confrontation this morning, Ann had retreated to the room she shared with Walter and hadn't emerged since. Dale wondered if she had told the old man already, part of him hoping that she had kept it to herself. Walter needed his strength in order to heal and get back on his feet. News like that would only derail that process.

"I think the stairs are great," Brooke said. "What's not so great is we haven't seen any other traders, apart from Billy, since the cartel attacked us."

Dale had noticed the same thing, but had told himself they would eventually return.

"There are items for the house we need," she said. "Stuff we normally exchanged for jugs of water. It was one of the reasons Sandy and I had to head to the Keller farm to find fertilizer. I just can't help but feel like each time we head off, we risk driving right into an ambush."

The thought made the flesh on Dale's scalp shrink-wrap to his skull. "We've been fortunate, I know. But I'm not sure what to tell you. If folks are too afraid to come by, what can we do?"

She glanced up at him. "Maybe if we talk to Billy, he could get the word out that things are safe, at least for now. I think it's also important people see that we're doing what we can to contribute."

Markets in war-torn Third World countries often operated even amid the sound of distant fighting. As US forces had discovered during patrols in Baghdad and the rest of Iraq, finding markets devoid of people was usually a sign of an ambush.

107

"If they aren't loyal to us," she went on, working her diplomatic magic on him, "they may become loyal to Sheriff Gaines or worse, the cartel."

The thought was indeed a frightening one. Besides, what Brooke was suggesting didn't involve a long drive. Billy was close enough that he often walked to their place.

"All right," Dale said at last. "I'll head over."

She cocked her head at an angle then drew her lips into a thin line.

"Fine, you can come too."

Regardless, it would need to be a quick visit, since he'd already begun work on the tunnel and wanted to get another few feet done before dinner. For that, he needed more two-by-fours and sheets of plywood to act as a brace against cave-ins. Perhaps heading to Billy's wasn't such a bad idea after all.

•••

After filling the pickup with six jugs of well water and arming themselves appropriately, Dale and Brooke headed out. The drive along Charleston was laughably short, perhaps a mile down the road on the way into town. A few more minutes and they would reach the school, the spot where Zach and his biker boys had been ambushed and slaughtered.

They pulled into Billy's driveway and killed the engine about the same time the crusty old guy appeared in the doorway, shotgun in hand and attitude aplenty. He had a quaint white bodega-style house, surrounded by all manner of junk. At one time, this might have been considered an eyesore. These days, it was a shopping center.

He squinted as Dale approached.

"Good to see you, Dale," he said. "Glad to see you brought your lovely daughter instead of that ill-tempered mutt."

"Duke would be hurt to hear you talk like that," Dale said, grinning.

"Well, he can kiss my grits." Billy laughed and then coughed violently into his closed fist. When he was done, he wiped his hand on the leg of his grease-stained jeans and fixed them with a sharp stair. "I know why you're here."

He must have seen the plastic bottles of water sloshing around on the bed of the truck.

"Yes, but not only for that," Dale admitted. "We couldn't help but notice no one's been by to trade recently. We wondered if you might spread the word that we're still very much alive and open for business."

Billy seemed to consider that as he set the shotgun against a chair. "Believe me, Dale, they know you're still around. That ain't the problem."

"Then what's keeping them away?" Brooke asked, jumping in.

"Looks just as beautiful as her mother, this one," Billy said, his tone respectful and brimming with nostalgia.

Dale put an arm around his daughter, who twisted out of his grasp. She wanted to be taken seriously and he admonished himself for letting his fatherly love transform her from the woman she'd become back into the little girl who used to cry to be picked up and cuddled.

"Well, Billy, you gonna answer the young lady?"

Billy's face darkened. "To put it simply, we been warned not to, Dale. Told by the sheriff and his deputies that trading with you is tantamount to an act of treason and I'm sure you can guess what the punishment for that is. The explosion this morning didn't help matters."

"Explosion?" Dale said, surprised.

"You haven't heard? Cartel brought in a handful of water trucks from across the border and someone went and blew 'em up. Last I heard, some folks thought it was you or that brother-in-law of yours."

"Zach?"

"Yep. He sure is a loaded pistol, that one."

Dale shook his head before the words were even out. "I don't know who did this, but I can assure you it wasn't any of us. These last few hours we've had our own problems to deal with."

"Oh, I know you weren't responsible," Billy told him flat out. "Minute I heard, I figured it was those idiots playing soldier. Think they're some kind of resistance movement, but I already told you they're nothing but a bunch of vandals. Apparently, that Ortega fella got so upset he executed a man in cold blood right after it happened. Said he'd do plenty more if those responsible weren't caught. Seems Sheriff Gaines is gonna have his hands full."

Following their chat, Dale convinced Billy to trade the wood he needed to help brace the tunnel. It was only after they were done, during that short drive home, that Brooke told him what had really happened at the Keller farm.

"Brooke, I can't believe you kept that from me," Dale said, feeling his mood darken even more. The feeling of being so far out of the loop wasn't a good one.

"I knew you'd only forbid me to set foot off the property again. You'd already convinced yourself Sandy and I couldn't take care of ourselves. Don't forget she was a sheriff's deputy."

Dale pulled in and then killed the engine. "I'm just thankful neither of you were hurt."

"Caleb would never do something like that."

"Caleb? The two of you are on a first-name basis now?"

She smiled. "We went to Encendido High together. He wanted our help, but I told him it was something you'd never want to get mixed up in."

"And you'd be right," Dale said, thoughtfully, slowly. "Except things have changed. You heard from Billy how the cartel executed a man. It won't be long before that isolated incident becomes a daily affair. It was one thing when we were dealing with Randy and Hugh, but now with the cartel killing innocent civilians, the situation's different."

"So you're saying you're not mad?"

He looked at her, the muscles in his face tense. "I'm saying maybe it's time you contact Caleb and tell him to set up a meeting with his boss."

Chapter 20

Not long after, Dale was upstairs knocking on the door to Walter and Ann's room. She opened the door a crack and poked her head out.

"Can I speak with you?" he asked.

Her eyes fell to her hands and hung there for a moment. "Is it about Nicole?"

He didn't respond, but he didn't need to because Ann already knew what this was about. She followed him into an empty room down the hall that Brooke and Colton were sharing.

"Have you told Walter yet?" He was referring to the situation with Nicole.

"I just don't have the heart to," she explained, her eyes welling up again. She rubbed them, trying to fight away the tears.

"I get that he's recovering and the timing isn't great," Dale began. "But we need to make a decision and I couldn't imagine doing that without speaking to him first."

Intellectually, she seemed to understand Dale's argument. Emotionally, however, the act of sitting down and having that gut-wrenching conversation with her husband was proving too spiny a subject to broach. Much like a rotting molar, the fear of short-term pain often made people endure long-term agony.

When she didn't say anything, Dale went on. "We should go in and talk to him together."

"When?" she asked quietly.

"Right now," he answered.

They left the privacy of that bedroom and headed back to where Walter was recuperating. Both of them entered and stood at the foot of his bed. The night table next to him was littered with rolls of fresh bandages and medical tape. Sitting next to that was a plastic cup with a bendy straw and a dog-eared paperback novel.

Walter opened his eyes and smiled briefly before the corners of his lips dropped into something resembling a frown.

"I've only seen that look on Ann's face one other time," Walter said. "It was spring of nineteen sixty-two and Doctor Cheevers was trying to tell us we would never have children of our own. I didn't believe him, not for a damn second, but the look on Ann's face then—it was like she somehow already knew."

"I wish we had better news for you, Walter," Dale said, the fingers of his left hand doing a nervous little dance, perhaps a carryover from a childhood dealing with overbearing parents and disgruntled schoolteachers.

"No one's dead, I hope," Walter said, using his elbows to prop himself up in bed.

Ann still wasn't saying anything and so Dale carried on. He explained what had happened the evening that he had discovered Nicole on the shortwave, speaking with Shane. Predictably, the old man's face had squished up with acute confusion. Walter sat in stunned silence for several minutes, his gaze drifting toward the window and a striking blue sky outside. Ann remained next to Dale, standing as rigid as a statue, not saying a word.

When he couldn't take it any longer, Dale finally said, "We've discussed what to do about this, but she's your daughter and I wanted to get both of your opinions before we made a move."

"Where is she?" Walter asked. "At the very least I'd like to talk to her, get her side of the story."

"She's already given it," Ann said. "Everything Dale told you is true and let me be the first of us to say that I not only disapprove of what Nicole has done, I hate it with all my heart. Dale opened up his house to us and this was how she repaid him. That's not the way we raised her."

Across the room, Walter sat, silently agreeing with his wife.

"Zach and the others haven't been shy about asking for her execution. I know as her mother you'll expect me to do everything in my power to save her life, but there has to be a way we can make up for this. There are so few of us against so many. It may not look it, but Walter taught both of us how to shoot a gun. Strictly speaking she isn't our blood, I know, but…"

Hearing Ann beg was making the situation so much harder.

"Doesn't matter a lick to me if Nicole was adopted or not," Walter cut in. "She's our daughter and I love her. But if she did what you're accusing her of, then she needs to pay for that."

"What do you recommend?" Dale asked.

"A secret vote," Walter replied. "Each of us fills out a ballot with one of three options. The highest number wins."

"And what shall we set as the terms of punishment?"

"Banishment," he said. "Rehabilitation or…" Walter paused. "Execution."

Dale nodded. "That sounds fair. And if they pick the last option? What then?"

Walter's eyes hardened. "Then I'll do it myself."

Ann's knees gave out and Dale caught her. "I'll get started right away," he said. "But I can tell you right now I don't see anyone voting for rehabilitation and for many of us, banishment feels like she'd be getting off easy."

"It is what it is," Walter replied stoically. "I fought North Koreans and Chinese forces who wanted nothing more than to put a bullet in my head, and yet this might be one of the hardest things I've ever had to face." He half smiled. "But when is doing the right thing ever easy, right?"

Dale agreed with his friend and left the room, certain he couldn't have said it better himself.

Chapter 21

Dale went outside to find Colton and Dannyboy out front, working on the trench nearest the driveway. Further down, Sandy and Brooke were hard at work doing the same while Zach was mending the fence the cartel had knocked over during their attack. He would speak to each of them one at a time, outlining his conversation with Walter as well as the importance of what they were doing. Nicole had conspired against them and they needed to vote their conscience on an appropriate punishment.

Zach was fiddling with a length of barbed wire when Dale finished.

"I don't need a paper," he said after the explanation was over. "You know as well I do that she needs to die."

"That may be so," Dale replied. "But everyone gets their say."

"We're a real democracy, aren't we?"

Dale didn't like his tone. "When it comes to making decisions of life and death, we sure are."

Zach removed his dirty work gloves, took the paper, wrote *death*, folded it over and then slid it into Dale's shirt pocket.

"We might not see eye to eye," Dale said, removing the scrap. "But I expect us to get along and respect one another. I won't put up with any less."

"Listen, I'm not trying to make a big deal," Zach replied. "For me, loyalty and trust are key. A person breaks that, they're as good as dead to me anyhow."

Dale had finally found something he and Zach could agree on. He clapped him on the shoulder and left to speak with Sandy and Brooke.

Both of them were unsettled by the notion of Nicole being killed.

"It's not like she actually put a gun to someone's head and pulled the trigger," Brooke said, staring down at the blank piece of paper.

"Maybe not," Dale retorted. "But just think if she'd gotten her way. All of us would either be dead, imprisoned or homeless."

"What if Shane put her up to it?" Sandy protested. "I mean, would that make her guilt as strong?"

"Shane is a lot of things," Dale told them. "But a mastermind he isn't. What they did took planning and determination. Those are not qualities Shane possesses."

Sandy leaned on her shovel and dabbed the sweat from her forehead. "So you're saying she manipulated your brother?"

"Even if only by stoking a flame that was already there. She's always been ambitious. Back when they were only dating, she was always riding Shane for never being successful enough. She was the one who convinced him to open that bar in town and after it failed, to become an electrician, and when that too went nowhere, she begged me to get him a job at Teletech. I did what I could and even that didn't last. His good looks could get him in the

117

door, but they couldn't keep him there. Listen, this isn't a court of law. I don't have any proof, but I've been thinking about it a great deal lately and I'm growing more and more convinced she was the one who first mentioned how Shane had gotten the raw end of the deal after our parents died."

"You make her sound like some kind of monster," Brooke said.

"I'm not trying to," Dale said truthfully. "In a way, Nicole was perfect for my brother. And under different circumstances she might have pushed him to accomplish something great. It's just too bad they chose the easy way."

"What did Walter say when you told him?" Sandy asked, saddened by the whole situation.

Dale shook his head. "Said if everyone voted for death, he'd do it himself."

The image clearly left both women feeling disturbed.

"How are you voting, Dad?" Brooke asked, squinting as she looked up into his eyes.

"I haven't decided just yet," he replied and that was also the truth.

He was about to walk away to let them figure it out when Brooke called him back. "You remember those feelers you wanted me to send out?"

"The resistance?"

She nodded. "I did as you said and found this on one of the posts by the road not long ago."

It was a note which read:

6:00 p.m. The abandoned public works depot. Don't be late.

Dale folded up the piece of paper and slipped it into his pocket, right beside Zach's vote.

"The three of us will go together," he said.

Brooke's eyes lit up.

Sandy was in the middle of telling them they should be careful, that they didn't know who these people were, when they heard the distinct sound of a single gunshot coming from around back.

Chapter 22

They raced around the house to find the retractable stairs had been lowered. Ten yards from the barn a body lay sprawled. Pistol in hand, Dale ran to the prone figure, turned it over and saw that it was Nicole. A single high-powered rifle round had torn through her chest, killing her instantly. His eyes traced up to the window next to the staircase and he saw that it was open, but also that it was empty. Dale ran up the steps, taking them two at a time before ducking in through the opening. Inside the southern bedroom he found his Remington 700 discarded on the floor, as though someone had thrown it down right after taking the shot. Three strides later he was in Walter and Ann's room. It seemed the old man had done what he had promised to do. Dale found the old couple sobbing in each other's arms.

"Why'd you do it?" Dale asked, still reeling.

Ann shook her head vigorously. "It was me," she said, her hands trembling. "I untied her and told her to run. She's in the Lord's hands now. Let Him be the one to judge her guilt."

Slowly, Dale left the room, closing the door behind him so they could have some privacy. A ghostly image of Brooke's face rose up before him. Dale couldn't imagine having to make that kind of decision. He hoped he never would.

•••

They laid Nicole to rest—Zach, Dannyboy and Colton conspicuously absent. Dale had to admit, it did seem strange voting on whether to execute someone for treason and then praying over their remains. But he wasn't doing it for her, he was doing it for Walter and for Ann.

After they were done, Dale, accompanied by Duke and Brooke, returned to the basement and carried on digging the tunnel, setting up braces every few feet and dragging out the loose earth. It would take a while longer, he knew, and when it was done, he would camouflage the entrance so that anyone who used it to escape wouldn't find themselves being caught like a rat in a hole. Telegraphing its location would defeat the entire purpose.

It was half past five when Sandy came down to get him.

"I'll give you two a minute," Brooke said, going upstairs for a drink of water.

"Geez, you're covered in dirt," Sandy said, holding him still while she shook dark granules of earth out of his hair. He closed his eyes, for a moment looking like a child being scolded for messing up his Sunday best. Duke snapped playfully at the falling debris.

"I appreciate it," Dale said, tilting his head to the left and knocking a few flecks from his ear.

"We should leave soon."

He pulled her in close and she closed her eyes, expecting a kiss. Instead, he squeezed her in a firm and loving hug. That was what he needed most at the moment. Dale wasn't the type to say much when things were troubling him. He was a man who believed words were cheap and that actions were the only currency that carried any real value.

They stayed like that for a minute, maybe more. He couldn't tell, but he'd meant what he said before. He appreciated everything Sandy had done, both big and small.

They found Zach waiting for them at the top of the basement stairs.

"You didn't think you were going to meet this guy without me, did you?"

"I wasn't sure you'd be interested," Dale said.

"Well, I am," he replied.

Dale and Sandy shared a look. Zach was unpredictable, but sometimes that could work to your advantage.

Shortly after, Dale, Zach, Sandy and Brooke piled into the front and back seats of the pickup. Needless to say they were well-armed and Dale was hopeful they would be able to skirt around the existing cartel checkpoints and positions with relative ease. The truth was, Edwardo didn't have the manpower yet to guard static sites. He apparently wanted his men to remain mobile and nimble.

The drive to the public works depot along the eastern outskirts of town took close to twenty minutes. Once there they found a large flat space enclosed by a series of concrete slabs. Inside were smaller areas where piles of gravel and sand were kept. To the right, a handful of dump trucks sat parked, each emblazoned with the town name.

"You sure this is right?" Zach asked from the back, searching in vain for signs of life.

Dale pulled the note from his pocket and read it again. "Seems that way. What time is it?"

"Five fifty-eight," Brooke replied.

They exited the pickup, weapons in the low ready position. A lone figure appeared near a squat beige building to the right. He drew nearer and Brooke whispered his name.

"Caleb?" Zack whispered back. He squared his shoulders. "Well, whoever he is, he looks twelve and a half."

Brooke elbowed her uncle. "He's my age and the only reason we're even here."

"I'd ask that you lower your weapons," Caleb said, now less than thirty feet away. "But somehow I don't think it'd do any good."

"Smart kid," Zach said, pointing a thumb in his direction.

"We know about the war you've been waging against local law enforcement as well as the cartel," Caleb began.

"They've been waging war on us," Dale corrected him. "We came here to meet your boss Nobel and I'm starting to wonder whether he was worth the effort."

Nobel emerged from behind a dump truck. "I'm glad you came." Sunglasses covered her eyes and a blue bandana the rest of her face. She came within a few feet and removed them both.

Zach rubbed his eyes. "You're a woman."

She stared Zach up and down. "Then it seems we have something in common."

"And sharp too," Sandy noted.

"My real name is Vickie, but when all of this first began, folks seemed more inclined to listen to someone

123

with a fancy code name." Her eyes flitted over the group and stopped at the end. "You must be Dale. It's a pleasure to finally meet you."

Once the introductions were squared away, Vickie explained how she'd formed the organization to fight against the growing autocracy in town, and how with the arrival of the cartel, her job had become so much more important and so much more dangerous. She then outlined her group's vision for Encendido's future.

"You don't expect Ortega and his men to just pack up and go home, do you?" Zach said with obvious derision.

Vickie wasn't impressed. "We have a plan in place," she began. "Someone important on the inside. But you'll forgive me if I don't share the details with people I just met."

"Does that plan involve destroying water trucks?" Dale asked.

"That wasn't us," she told them. "I was getting to that. There's another movement headquartered in an old Baptist church under a man named Calvin, and let's just say they've started pushing back against the cartel and anyone who supports them. They want them dead and gone, no matter the collateral damage. We don't want our town turned into a war zone and I've been trying to reel him in."

"Or maybe you could let him do his thing," Zach said, rolling up the sleeves of his shirt. "If you're sitting back and hoping the bad guys suddenly find Jesus, we could be waiting around for a long time."

If Vickie didn't like Zach earlier, she was hating him now.

"Listen," Zach went on, "I just think the passive approach never got anyone anywhere."

"It's even harder to get anywhere when you and the people around you are dead," she replied sternly. "We want lasting change. There's no point trading one dictator for another."

"She's got a point," Dale piped up. "All I want is for my family and me to be left in peace."

Vickie fixed him with her deep brown eyes. "Believe me, that's something we all want. But you can see now that standing on the sidelines isn't an option anymore. If not you wouldn't be here."

Dale nodded. "What can we do to help?"

"That depends. There may be times when some of our agents will need a safehouse, a place to lie low for a few hours or even days. We could also use some resources—"

"I see where this is going." Dale cut her off. "You need water."

She nodded.

"How much?"

"As much as you can spare," Vickie told him. "I could also use someone like you on our side."

Dale grew quiet while Zach looked offended at being excluded.

"I'm not a soldier," Dale told her straight up. "I'm a farmer, a family man, and I'd like to keep it that way."

She wasn't buying it. "You held off more than one attack when you were outnumbered and probably outgunned."

"Not without losses," he said, his mind going to Shane and Nicole and the festering wound their deception had left. "I'll do what I can to help, but for now, let's keep it at that."

Vickie put her glasses and bandana back on. "We'll be in touch," she said enigmatically and left.

Dale watched her go, wondering if she was Encendido's best hope or another townsperson obsessed with playing soldier who would only get innocent people killed.

125

Chapter 23
Zach

Zach spent the rest of the evening mulling over what Vickie—or Nobel—had told them, all the while formulating a plan of his own. The next morning, after breakfast, he told Colton and Dannyboy to meet him in the barn out back. The air inside was cool and a nice contrast to the stifling heat under the baking sun. It looked like the thermometer would push a hundred and ten degrees today. Zach was beginning to appreciate the hardships his ancestors had suffered, trying to tame a wild and unforgiving landscape. In those old pictures you could see how outdoor work had left their skin a deep shade of brown. By contrast, his time in Florence Supermax had left him pasty and nearly translucent. Only now was he starting to get some color back.

"You gonna finally tell us how it went yesterday?" Dannyboy asked, upset Zach had opted to keep them both in the dark so long.

"She hated me," Zach began, not bothering with any kind of context.

"Who hated you?" Colton asked, confused.

126

Zach paused, collecting himself. Some folks were great at telling stories—knew exactly where to start and how to ratchet up to a riveting climax. Zach wasn't one of those people. He tended to rely on the sheer force of his character to keep those around him following what he was saying. He started at the beginning, telling them all about the meeting with Nobel and her vision of a liberated Encendido, then about the explosion and how some other group had been responsible for it.

"Sounds to me like she's all talk and no action," Dannyboy said with disgust.

"So what's this other group that blew up those water trucks?" Colton wondered.

Zach raised an index finger between them. "That's where I was heading to, if you'd give me a chance to get there, son."

Colton's expression changed noticeably, but not in reaction to being scolded by Zach. He was beaming with joy at hearing his father call him *son* for the first time in years.

Zach hesitated before continuing. "There's another group operating out there who seem to think along the same lines we do and have already started taking the fight to the enemy."

"So what are you suggesting?" Dannyboy asked.

"Nobel said they were holed up in an abandoned Baptist church," Zach told them.

"That's south of town," Colton said.

Zach's eyes lit up. "Praise the Lord. Grab a few weapons, boys. We're going for a drive."

∙∙∙

Minutes later, they were in the Brinks truck, gunning past the school, taking a screeching left on Del Sol Avenue toward the southern end of town.

127

"What did Dale say when you told him we were leaving?" Colton asked.

Zach and Dannyboy burst into laughter. "We're grown men and we come and go as we please."

"I know that," Colton said, backpedaling slightly. "I was just saying."

"Let's get one thing straight," Zach said, shifting gears on the large armored truck. "Dale's doing his best to turn you into his clone and I'm not having it. He's not a bad guy—fact, he was there for you when I was locked up—but you're a Baird, not a Hardy, and don't you forget that."

Colton nodded, although he didn't seem entirely convinced. It was easy for Zach to talk tough, but even he had to admit to being away for the most important part of his son's life. The thought tore at Zach often and in ways he wasn't prepared to let on to anyone. That guilt was part of why he'd rushed home from Colorado the minute the opportunity presented itself. If he couldn't change the past, then he'd sure as hell work to change the future.

They pulled onto Baker Street and found the area about as deserted as the rest of the town. It was hard to believe sometimes there were nearly three thousand folks still eking out an existence in Encendido. Seemed many of them had gone underground, both literally and figuratively.

The homes here showed fewer signs of vandalism and disrepair. Was this because they were still occupied or had the roving gangs of looters not made it this far? A sign on a front lawn answered their question.

Anyone caught looting or trespassing will be shot on sight!

"These people mean business," Zach said, leaning over the giant wheel as they cruised down the street.

"We might be making the wrong impression," Colton said.

"How so?" Dannyboy said, as though he found the very notion personally offensive.

Colton looked through one of the side windows, the bulletproof glass turning the world beyond into something out of a carnival house of mirrors. "This truck probably looks to them like a tank. Something Sheriff Gaines or the cartel might go around in."

Dannyboy nodded. "Kid does have a point."

The comment made Colton laugh. "Kid? You're only a year older than I am and I'm twice your size."

"Boys, stop fighting," Zach called from the driver's seat. "Don't make me pull over." He turned and winked at Colton. The family drive from hell. They sure were making up for lost years.

"On your right," Dannyboy called out when he spotted the church, a quaint white structure topped by a tall white spire.

"We're about to enter the Lord's house, boys," Zach said. "Hope your souls are clean."

He pulled the truck into the parking lot around back, each of them searching for any sign of life, threatening or otherwise.

Dannyboy stood up in the narrow confines of the truck, his shotgun in both hands. "You know those zombie movies where the hero thinks he's found a safe place and then gets swarmed by an army of undead?"

"Uh, sort of," Colton replied, suddenly looking even more uncomfortable.

Dannyboy leaned in. "Well, this is that movie." He racked his shotgun.

Colton flinched and stumbled backward. Dannyboy burst into gales of laughter.

"Lock and load, boys," Zach said. "We're going in. And in case it wasn't already obvious, neither of you says a word. Leave the talking to me."

Chapter 24

The three men were no sooner out of the truck than a disembodied voice told them to freeze. Zach glanced around and saw a fence line that divided the houses beyond church property. A rifle crack pierced the air, the round dinging off the Brinks truck a few inches from the roof. Zach swung around and swore when he saw the dent.

"Weapons on the ground and your hands in the air," the voice ordered them. He was hiding somewhere behind the fence.

Zach did as they were instructed, motioning for the other two to follow suit. When he was bent over, laying his pistol on the ground, he whispered to Dannyboy. "I like these guys already."

Two men came rushing out from the church, carrying a pair of Kel-Tec SU-16s. The first guy was dressed in cargo shorts with a green military-style t-shirt, the other torn jeans and a white shirt.

A moment later, the sniper from behind the fence emerged into the open. He was decked in full camo and carried a Ruger American hunting rifle.

"You nearly shot us with that piece of junk?" Zach barked, insulted.

The sniper glanced down at his rifle and shrugged. "Woulda done the job if you'd tried something stupid."

"They look like scavengers to me," said the one in the khaki shorts. His arms were well muscled, but his legs were skinny.

"We aren't scavengers, but you do need to change your workout program," Zach observed. "Those twigs you call legs aren't doing you any favors."

Colton nudged him. His son seemed worried they were about to get their heads blown off, but Zach knew what he was doing. These guys had to see they weren't afraid, that they belonged here, maybe even owned the place.

The one with the jeans collected the weapons they placed on the asphalt. His arms full, he said, "So far all you've done is sling insults. That isn't good for a man's health."

"I call it like I see it," Zach replied. He reached behind him and all three men aimed their guns at him. "Relax, boys, it's eight hundred degrees out here and my shirt's starting to feel like a second skin. Any chance we can take this party inside?"

They looked from one to another, not sure what to make of their brash new visitor.

•••

Zach and the others were led into the church and a side staircase which led to the basement. Two flights later, they entered a dim room, brimming with activity. The windows had been boarded up and in some cases covered over with black paint. Light from candles and battery-powered lanterns gave the place a ghostly feel. Men wearing tactical vests and armed with pistols moved from one area to another. They seemed to be analyzing pictures and Zach wondered if these were part of further attacks they were planning against law enforcement and the cartel.

From out of the gloom, an imposing figure approached. He was tall, six foot two, maybe taller, with broad shoulders and hands the size of catcher's mitts.

"They pulled right up to the back door in an armored truck," the man in khakis reported. He fished a wrapped candy out of his pocket and popped it in his mouth. "We intercepted and disarmed them before they could get inside."

The tall man nodded. "Good job, Travis."

"Quite an operation you got here, Calvin," Zach said to the tall guy he assumed was their leader.

His eyes narrowed. "Have we met before?" From out of the darkness, a man came and whispered into Calvin's ear. "Ah, you're Dale Hardy's men."

"We're nobody's men," Zach corrected him. "Dale's my brother-in-law, but that doesn't make him my boss."

"I was going to say that your reputation precedes you, but you don't look like a man who enjoys flattery." Calvin had read Zach well.

"I like results. When I heard there was a crew willing to trade blows with the cartel, I knew we had to meet."

"So you want to join us?" Calvin asked, eyeing them over. "We could always use more men and women willing to fight for our cause. But first, I'll need something from you. Call it a sign of good faith."

Zach folded his arms. "This is normally where you take a perfectly good thing and mess it up."

"You don't like authority," Calvin said, fixing him with a dark set of eyes. "And that can make you hard to control."

"I don't take well to orders," Zach replied. "Everyone here has come to you as an equal, offering their help to overthrow the cartel. I'm no different, but I won't be made to feel like a grunt."

"Fair enough," Calvin said. "I'm happy to have you join the cause. But your farm sits on the largest working aquifer in the county and water just happens to be the one thing we need most."

"First off, what you need most are better weapons if you want any chance of going toe to toe with Ortega's men. Second, it isn't my farm, and getting a drop of water out of Dale is about as easy as drawing blood from a stone."

"Five hundred gallons," Calvin said. "Consider it an admittance fee."

"I didn't come here to follow," Zach said squarely. "I came here to lead this group of ragtag misfits. You may need drinkable water, but what you need more is a real leader. One who knows what the hell he's doing."

One of the guards moved in but was waved off by Calvin. "Is that right?"

The other members of Calvin's underground movement had stopped what they were doing and began to gather around.

Now it was Zach's turn to stare his opponent down. It didn't matter that the guy had three or four inches on him. Zach suffered from what a fellow inmate at Florence Supermax called Chihuahua syndrome. Not because he was a yappy dog, but because little dogs often had no idea how small they really were. Likewise, Zach didn't mind in the slightest fighting a man twice his size. But as much as his fists were itching for a little exercise, he knew throwing down here and now with all these armed men standing around was not a good idea. Instead, he decided to throw another kind of jab. "You outed yourself as an amateur the minute you blew those water trucks up instead of snatching them right from under the cartel's noses. You're out of your depth,

Calvin. I'm here to throw you a life preserver, help you get to shore before you drive the town's only shot at freedom straight off a cliff."

"We don't need your help," Calvin barked, and for the first time, Zach could see he'd touched a nerve. Cracks were beginning to appear in the tall man's otherwise impenetrable edifice. More importantly, he could see the look of doubt creeping into the faces of the men standing around them. He had planted a deadly seed and he knew with time that seed would germinate. The real question was, how long would it take?

"Hand us our weapons and we'll be on our way then," Zach said.

Travis looked at Calvin, who said, "They'll be waiting for you outside, by your truck. But if I see you snooping around here again, you won't get a warning shot next time."

Zach had about five great comebacks lined up, but chose to stay quiet. Watching Calvin come groveling for him to change his mind was all the satisfaction he would need.

Chapter 25
Randy

Encendido wasn't known for its greenery. Few could be accused of describing the town as lush with vegetation. What existed in its place were stunted-looking plants and trees, adapted to living in a bitter environment, surviving off the few drops of rainwater which fell each year. So in 2010, when the council had voted to build a four-acre park near the center of town, in part to fill the space vacated by a defunct strip mall, it had seemed like a great idea. Little had they known then that a few short years later, the now dried and parched grass which carpeted the grounds would house an executioner's scaffold.

The wooden structure smacked of something out of an old spaghetti western. A set of stairs led up to a gangplank where eight nooses hung at equal distances from one another. Except right now, none of those eight nooses were dangling free. They were cinched around the necks of six men and two women.

Four of the men had been picked up at a cartel checkpoint, driving in a vehicle witnesses claimed had shot at a sheriff's deputy. But their first mistake, Randy realized, was travelling around four to a car. The cartel had recently passed a law that stipulated no more than three men could assemble at any one location, inside a vehicle or otherwise. The penalty for noncompliance was death. It was designed to dissuade the overly civic-minded citizens from taking to the streets in protest, which explained the rest of the executions slated for that day. There would be more tomorrow, depending on Edwardo's mood and how lenient or bloodthirsty he felt at the moment in question.

Lately, there hadn't been much in the way of leniency. Not since the bombing of his water trucks and the humiliating call he'd been forced to make to his father south of the border. Like Roman governors in the ancient world, Edwardo had been sent to rule this new part of his father's kingdom. And like that long-ago era, acts of rebellion were met with justice that was both brutal and swift. Swift because instead of a trial, Edwardo, in his infinite wisdom, had judged the accused himself and come to what he declared was a flawless and infinitely fair decision. Death.

There was no longer room for dissent in this world Randy found himself operating in. So he had gone along with it. Better to be chasing away a nagging conscience than swinging from the end of a rope.

Much to his surprise, a crowd had gathered to watch the spectacle, perhaps more out of curiosity and disgust than anything else. The population was divided by acts of kindness and terror and as such they had become easier to control. And yet some opposition was occurring with greater frequency. It was almost as though the bombs which had destroyed those water trucks had awakened something inside people, giving them permission to stand up and say no. But the more they did just that, the more Edwardo's anger turned to rage. There was at least one fairly well-organized resistance movement, but finding them wasn't as easy as it sounded, even in a town the size of Encendido. Patrol cars had to pair up, sometimes driving in threes to avoid ambushes. The town was starting to boil over and Randy was certain the executions Edwardo had planned in the coming days would only make things worse.

A large number of the cartel enforcers were here, along with Edwardo himself, who moved next to Randy. He seemed agitated, tapping the grip of his pistol while his eyes darted around.

"I'll be calling my father tonight," Edwardo said and Randy suddenly understood the reason for the cartel lieutenant's nerves.

"To tell him how the executions went?" Randy guessed.

Edwardo shook his head. "To ask him to send in La Brigada de Los Asesinos."

Randy didn't have a clue what he was talking about, although their name translated loosely into 'the killers brigade.' "They sound serious."

Edwardo cackled. "You don't know the half of it. Just as the SS had the lightning bolts, La Brigada have the skull and bones to strike fear in people's hearts. One time, my father was having trouble with a little town called Cuauhtemoc. The people there didn't want to pay him taxes anymore. He'd already bribed every member of the police force, but they became outnumbered by a militia the town had assembled to protect the people. They left him with no choice but to summon La Brigada."

Randy felt the hairs stand up on the back of his neck. "What happened to the town?"

"They fought back," Edwardo said, his eyes scanning the scaffold and the men and women who were waiting to die. "Big mistake, my friend."

The executioner looked at Edwardo, who flicked his hand in the air, giving him the sign. A lever was pulled and eight trap doors snapped open. The men and women dropped, stopping violently, their legs dangling like marionettes.

Edwardo grinned. "Sooner or later your people will learn to accept my authority. I just hope when that happens a few of them will still be left alive." He walked away then, surrounded by his bodyguard and the rest of his men.

"What should we do with the bodies?" Randy called after him, eyeing the dead with a sickening feeling as he watched them swing back and forth.

"Leave them for now," Edwardo said. "A reminder to those who are tempted to resist."

A moment later, Deputy Keith appeared.

"I need you to do something for me," Randy said, his eyes fixed on the scaffold and the cruel work it had just completed.

"Sure thing."

"You remember Betty Wilcox?"

"Joe's sister? She used to be the head nurse."

"Yeah, she was taken by two men. I need you to find out where they took her." Randy nodded at the scaffold and the implication was perfectly clear.

"All right," Keith said. "I'll see what I can do." He left, moving away at a decent clip.

It wasn't an exaggeration to say that Encendido was a town under siege. For many, Randy included, it had become a hell on earth—a mini-North Korea nestled in the American Southwest. But Randy had a sinking feeling all this would look like child's play compared to how things would be when La Brigada arrived.

Chapter 26

Dale emerged from the basement and the tunnel he'd been carving out these last few days, eager to fill his canteen, when he heard the sound of Duke barking. His hand went to the pistol at his side as he exited the garage and spotted a handful of traders standing at the end of his driveway.

"Easy, boy," he told the dog, ruffling the fur on his head.

He waved them forward, his spirits beginning to rise. It seemed Billy had been true to his word and convinced some of them to return. A middle-aged neighbor named Pam Steiger was the first in line, pulling a cart laden with several five-gallon containers of gasoline she'd likely scrounged from abandoned cars. After verifying its quality and adding stabilizer, Dale would use it to replenish the fifty-gallon tank he kept in the barn.

Next was David Halper, a former accountant who had lost his entire family to the virus. Dale had seen him before and knew trading offered the man a chance to get out of the house and spend time with other human beings once in a while. David had become quite handy at woodworking and brought some foldable chairs with a fine lacquered finish.

As per usual, the other members of Dale's household—save for Colton, Zach and Dannyboy—stopped what they were doing and picked over the items for sale, selecting what they wanted. When they were finished, Dale and the traders would then haggle over how many jugs were owed. Only after reaching an agreement would the water be poured and the transaction completed.

To an outsider, it might have appeared as though Dale was being cheap, trying to fleece these folks, but the truth was, haggling had become part of the social etiquette, an opportunity to engage in a sort of verbal chess game. It was a form of entertainment really. In a world without reality television and superhero movies, was it any surprise? But more than that, it was an opportunity for people to exchange information. Dale heard from each of them how the cartel's grip on the town was tightening, how they had begun a reign of terror where citizens were executed for the slightest infraction.

The real irony was that it made the time Mayor Reid and Sheriff Randy were in charge seem so much tamer. Not that those two wouldn't have eventually fallen down the same slippery slope that always seemed to lead from dictatorship to full-blown tyranny. It would only have taken a little longer.

Dale handed each of them a list of the things he was looking for; ammunition (9mm, .30-06 and .223), gasoline, two-by-fours and plywood as well as the types of toiletries that always seemed to be in short supply around the house. And with that, he left Sandy, Brooke and Ann to continue chatting and see them off when they were done.

Dale cut through the backyard, moving past the chicken coop and the vegetable garden, and headed toward the barn. There he found Zach, Colton and Dannyboy engaged in a heated, but hushed conversation. They stopped as soon as Dale entered the cool interior.

"Looks like I'm interrupting something," he said. There was a conspiratorial mist that hung in the air, and Dale didn't like the feel of it.

"We were only talking," Colton replied, looking decidedly nervous.

"Whispering was more like it," Dale corrected him. "If there's something on your mind, how about we get it out in the open?"

"We've tried that," Zach said, turning to face him. "And nothing changes. The situation is getting worse. And we can't afford to sit on our hands any longer. There are groups forming around town already," Zach went on, "committed to solving the problem."

"And I'm doing my part," Dale countered, defensively. "What are you doing?"

"The one thing you seem incapable of."

"Really, Zach? And what is that?"

"Taking the fight to the enemy."

Dale shook his head. "You need a steady hand for that sorta thing or innocent people will get hurt. What worked at Florence Supermax won't work in Encendido."

"My questionable ways didn't seem to bother you when Ortega's men were heading this way," Zach spat. "No, you were more than happy to have my help then."

"You don't have a clue what you're talking about."

"Oh, really?"

"I took you in for Colton's sake," Dale replied, hating what Zach was making him say in front of everyone, especially the man's own son. "I wasn't going to let you get slaughtered on our front lawn when you're all he's talked about for years. I may be quick to protect my family, but I'm not nearly as heartless as you think I am."

"When the dust settles, what side of history do you want to be on? The one that stayed safe in your castle or the one that put its neck on the line?"

Dale felt his blood pressure really begin to rise. "In case you've forgotten, I was the first and only one standing up to Sheriff Gaines and the mayor when they were busy snatching up everything they could get their hands on. I don't remember anyone coming to offer me help. If that looks like sitting on my hands, then we have very different definitions."

"I aim to get things done," Zach said, putting his arms around Colton and Dannyboy. "And I'm asking for your support."

"Get things done?" Dale repeated incredulously. "You still haven't shaken the impulse problem that landed you in Florence in the first place. Seems every time you turn around you're going off half-cocked, leaping in with both feet without giving a hoot where you're gonna land or who gets hurt. You don't get things done, Zach, you get people killed. Don't believe me? Ask the nineteen bikers who followed you into that ambush when you wouldn't listen to reason."

Zach's face was a mask of anger. He looked like he wanted to fight and might have if Brooke hadn't showed up.

"What's going on?" she asked, scared.

Dale and Zach were locked in a staring contest, neither man daring to blink first.

"Nothing," Dale answered finally. "We were just talking."

"We heard you shouting from out front."

"Your dad and I were having a discussion, is all," Zach explained. "We both feel very strongly. Just so happens our views don't quite match up."

"Well, you need to come inside," Brooke said. "A call's come through for you on the shortwave."

Dale looked at her, noting the distressed look on his daughter's face. "Who is it?"

She hesitated a moment before answering. "Shane."

Chapter 27

Sandy

Sandy was taking a break from the trench out front, tilting back a cup of cool water, when she saw Dale hurry past her and disappear into the house. She called after him but he didn't turn or respond. Brooke soon followed.

"Hey, what's going on?"

Brooke skidded to a stop just as Ann was coming out to tend to the garden. The two women nearly collided. Brooke hurried back to where Sandy was standing near the pumphouse. "It's Shane," she whispered, not wanting Ann to hear. "He's on the shortwave downstairs. Asked to talk to Dale."

"Oh, boy," Sandy said, her brow furrowing. "What I wouldn't give to be a fly on the wall for that conversation."

A noise by the driveway and a bark from Duke immediately drew their attention. Instinctively, Sandy's and Brooke's hands went for the pistols on their belts, both women looking like a Charlie's Angels poster. A white car sat idling by the road while Duke paced back and forth, yapping away.

A man in a deputy's uniform got out and waved Sandy over.

"Who the heck is that?" Brooke asked, her weapon drooping.

"It's Keith," Sandy said. "And he looks like he's got something to say." He was also clearly frightened of Duke. Given what the dog had done to his man parts, that wasn't a big surprise.

"Wait here," Sandy said and headed down the driveway toward Keith, the pistol still gripped tightly in her hand. When she got to within twenty feet she said, "You sure got guts showing up here."

He smiled weakly. "It's not what you think. I didn't come to start anything."

The two of them had always been on relatively good terms in spite of him being one of Randy's lackeys.

"Is there somewhere we can talk?" he asked.

"What's wrong with this?" Duke was still barking in the distance.

Keith glanced up at the blaring sun. "How about we sit in the car at least? No funny business, I swear. I'll even let you hold the keys. There's something important we need to discuss and there isn't any time to waste."

She took his car keys, slid them into her pocket and both of them sat in the car, the doors ajar. Beads of sweat rolled down Keith's face. The armpits and neckline of his shirt were soaked.

"You need a towel," she told him.

He reached his hand past her toward the glove compartment. She leveled the pistol. He motioned with his eyes. "Can I?" There was something in there he wanted to get.

"No tricks," she said. "This isn't a squirt gun I'm holding."

"I've seen you on the range," Keith said, opening the small door and pulling out a white hand towel. He ran it over his face and neck then let it plop in his lap. "You could plug a nickel at thirty feet."

"So you came here to woo me with flattery, is that it?" From the corner of her eye, Sandy saw that Brooke was still watching them. "Did Randy send you?"

Keith shook his head. "Randy's got much bigger fish to fry at the moment. He thinks I'm trying to track down Betty Wilcox."

"What a surprise that is," Sandy said. "You might not know the truth, but when Dale charged into the station looking for me, it was because I'd figured out Randy and Hugh Reid had some serious blood on their hands."

"They killed Joe and his wife and at least two others including Mayor Curtis Long. Yes, I know."

Hearing Keith's admission was shocking.

"But back then I didn't," he went on. "As far as I was concerned, the sheriff and the mayor were doing the best they could with the crappy hand fate had dealt them. That was before the cartel showed up. Before Nobel's people reached out and showed me the error of my ways."

Sandy was speechless.

"And I know why Randy wants to see the head nurse up on that scaffold, swinging from a noose. She's got proof that he's a murderer. He figures if he can survive the cartel, he'll have a chance at regaining his dominance over Encendido. Living through the cartel's occupation is his short-term goal. Killing Betty is part of the long-term one. But I know exactly where Betty is. She's with Nobel and her people, safe, at least for the time being."

Sandy was still stuck on something Keith had said moments earlier. "They've built a scaffold?" she said, the horror spilling into her voice.

He nodded. "And used it. Eight killed today. Who knows how many tomorrow. The charges are ginned up of course, but most have to do with one form of resistance or another. Edwardo needs to be locked up in an institution or somewhere on death row. Instead he's ruling over three thousand survivors from the greatest plague man has ever known."

"So why have you come to me?"

"Nobel's people are planning a major assault," he told her. "They wanna clear the cartel out of town once and for all."

"Then why don't they?"

"They aren't strong enough, not by themselves. It's not just a question of getting volunteers. Vickie needs people who know what they're doing. Folks who can handle a weapon and know how to move through a battlefield."

"Sounds like you need the 101st," Sandy said. "Wish I didn't have to be the one to tell you you're out of luck."

"When you spoke to Nobel," he said, brushing aside the dark-humored jab, "she told you that a man named Calvin Pike had grown his own resistance movement."

"She did. Said they were getting out of control."

Keith picked up the towel and dried his forehead. "She was right. Tactically, they're proficient, but Calvin hasn't a clue what he's doing. His operations have already killed a handful of townspeople, who just so happen to be the one group we can't afford to alienate. Without their cooperation and support the fight will be lost before it begins."

"I heard about the water trucks," Sandy said. "But I didn't realize that was him."

"Nobel needs Calvin's help if we want any chance at taking on the cartel."

"I'm assuming she's spoken to him."

Keith gave her a look. "The guy thinks he's Davy Crockett or something. He's tall, but most of that is propped up by ego more than anything."

"You want me to talk to him?" she asked. "Is that what you're asking?"

Keith's eyes darted away. "Calvin's a chauvinist and you're a strong woman. If you went, he would only waste time trying to prove his dominance over you."

"Sounds like a real catch for some lucky lady out there," Sandy said, feeling bile rise up in her throat.

"We were hoping you could convince Dale to go."

"Dale?"

"He's well known and well respected by the townsfolk," Keith said.

"Dale might find what you say hard to swallow."

"He's humble, but it's the truth. If he was able to reach out and help to broker a peace treaty, then the attack plan might actually have a shot at succeeding."

Sandy glanced out the window as she considered everything Keith had told her. "I'll think about it," she said at last, stepping out and tossing Keith his keys.

"Don't think about it too long," Keith said as she closed the passenger door. "Our window of opportunity is closing fast. Edwardo's about to call in reinforcements—the worst of the worst, apparently—and if he does that, it will tip the balance too far in his favor."

Keith's words continued echoing in her ears as he started the car, made a U-turn and sped back toward town. A clock was ticking somewhere inside her mind and with each beat she felt her own noose cinching tighter and tighter.

Chapter 28

Dale

Dale sat facing the shortwave radio, his muscles tense with a vortex of swirling emotion. Feelings that ranged from hatred for what his brother had done, to sadness that he would probably never see him again. He drew in a long breath and let it whistle out between his teeth. When he was done, Dale leaned into the mic and pressed the actuator. "Shane?"

Static, followed by silence. Then a weak voice answered. "It's good to hear your voice."

"I'm busy, Shane, so unless you're gonna start with an apology and something approaching an explanation, then I suggest you stop wasting my time."

"You always were one tough nut," Shane said. "Guess that's why Dad liked you best."

"Funny you see it that way when you were the one they gave most of the attention to."

"I was a screw-up," Shane said, a sense of sadness and yearning in his voice.

"There you go again, talking in the past tense. You never stopped screwing up, no matter how much Ma and

Pa struggled to pick up after you. Sure, the old man talked tough, but he never let you hit rock bottom, get the taste of what you deserved. Far as I see it, that's where they went wrong. They loved you too much, Shane, to let you fail, and you repaid their love by expecting them to be there whenever things got tough."

"You're right," Shane said and Dale was stunned by the admission, but also suspicious. Was this part of the sweet boy act that had worked so well on his parents, the same one he was now trying on Dale? Mess up as bad as you wanted so long as you could cock your head back and bat your eyelashes like an innocent child who didn't know any better.

"I don't care about being right, Shane. Much as you might find that hard to believe, all I ever wanted was for you to pull your head out of your backside and man up."

"I was so filled with resentment," his brother said. "It got so I couldn't see straight."

"Was that before or after Nicole started whispering in your ear?"

"She had nothing to do with it," Shane said, his voice tightening from the lie.

"That's not what she said when we interrogated her."

"Interrogated?" Shane said the words quietly, as though he were afraid to utter them.

"Imagine my surprise when I found the two of you talking late one night."

"She asked me about the weather and it was such a strange thing to say. I worried then that she'd been caught, I just didn't want to face the possibility. I know I messed up, but it's not too late to make this right," Shane protested. "I wanna come back."

"Of course you do," Dale replied, trying hard to subdue his growing anger and disgust. The English language didn't contain enough curse words to express what he wanted to say right now. "That sense of sadness

151

you're feeling—it's nothing but self-pity and disappointment that your plan backfired so spectacularly. Did you really think I would risk everyone's life?"

"I should have known better. But I'll make it up to you, Dale, I swear."

Dale felt his pulse quicken. "Listen, there's something you need to know. Nicole is dead."

"What?"

"I won't go into detail, but let's just say she was shot, trying to escape."

There was a long silence where Dale assumed his brother was either crying or trying to collect himself. Finally he spoke:

"Tell everyone I'm sorry, that I never meant for things to turn out this way."

"They'll never forgive you, Shane."

"I know," he replied. "What about you?"

Dale wasn't sure how to answer that. "I can't say just yet. Forgiveness and acceptance are two vastly different beasts. Hanging your family out to dry for your own gain, well, that's about as low as a person can get."

"I guess I finally hit that bottom you've always talked about."

Dale was alone in the darkened basement, nodding to himself. "I guess you have."

"You think there's anywhere up from here?"

Shane sounded hopeful and Dale remembered the little boy, caught by his mother stealing a cookie before dinner, her heart melting because he was just so darn cute. Then something else occurred to Dale, a chance for his brother to seek some form of redemption for what he'd done. "Are you alone?"

"What do you mean?"

"Not metaphorically alone. Is there anyone else in the room with you?"

"No, there isn't," Shane replied. "Why?"

"Because there may be a way you can start to set things right."

"Anything," Shane said. "I'll do all the outdoor work around the house for a month—no, for a year."

"Nah, nothing like that. You at the sheriff's office?"

"Yeah."

"I'll bet they're keeping you alive because they think you'll be able to get intel out of us, maybe even soften us up a little."

"I have no idea what they're thinking," Shane said. "To be honest, when the plan went bad I figured I was dead."

"You are," Dale said, unable to ignore the sting he felt hearing his brother talk about his plan like he was talking about a trip that got cancelled. "But there may be a way you can bring yourself back to life."

"I'm listening."

"In the next twenty-four hours I'm gonna get you a weapon and you're going to use that weapon to assassinate Edwardo Ortega."

"Oh, man," was Shane's only reply. "That sounds way too dangerous."

"You said anything. Well, there it is. You do that and the cartel will surely start to crack. Afterward it won't take more than a small push for it to fall over and shatter into a million little pieces."

Chapter 29
Zach

Zach, Colton and Dannyboy went out to make sure the booby-traps were still in working order. Zach paused to lean on his shovel and watch the ground in the distance shimmering from the heat.

"Hey," Colton said excitedly, not far from him. "Look at this."

Glancing over, he watched his son stoop down and pluck a large flat rock from the ground. One of the sides was painted with a green bullseye. Zach recognized it at once as the symbol used by Calvin and his merry band of men for their well-intentioned, but largely inept resistance movement. For a brief second, Zach wondered if this was meant to be some sort of threat or warning. Then Colton turned the rock over and showed him that scrawled underneath was the word: *Barn.*

Zach's AR was leaning against the porch. "You two stay here," he told Colton and Dannyboy before circling around back. A few moments later, Zach entered the barn.

"You got guts," he said aloud to no one in particular. "Sneaking around these parts, a man's liable to get himself shot."

"It's a risk I was willing to take," a disembodied voice replied from the shadows. It didn't sound like Calvin, but maybe he'd sent someone else to do his groveling.

"Who are you?" Zach asked, leveling the rifle at a patch of shadow.

"I'm surprised you don't recognize my voice." The figure stepped into the light.

"Travis?"

The man nodded. He was still wearing the same khaki shorts and green shirt.

"If Calvin's got something to say, I suggest he says it himself."

"That's not likely," Travis said. "Calvin's dead."

The news smacked Zach across the face like a sack filled with bricks. "Wasn't expecting that."

"There was a raid on one of our safehouses and Calvin was killed. Someone tipped them off. At least the gangly bastard went down fighting," Travis said. "I'll give him that."

"Gangly or not, he should never have been leading your outfit," Zach said. "I hate to speak ill of the dead, but he barely had one oar in the water, if you know what I mean."

"That's why I've come," Travis said. "We need someone to take over for him. Someone who can inspire the men. Who knows what he's doing."

Zach was brimming with plans and strategies, but more than that, he was bursting with confidence. It didn't matter that he'd never served in the military or led men into battle, unless you included the time he'd fought his way out of an ambush. He had a sort of magnetism that drew folks toward him, made them pay attention when he spoke and do as he said.

"This sure isn't the way I imagined it happening," Zach said. "But I accept." Shaking Travis' hand, he thought about Dale and how his brother-in-law would accuse him of abandoning the farm. "I'll need a few hours to get some things together."

"Of course," Travis said.

"And I'll be bringing some folks with me." He was thinking of Colton and Dannyboy.

"That's fine too. I'm just happy you said yes."

Zach started to walk away and then stopped. "That call to the authorities that got Calvin killed, that was you, wasn't it?"

Travis' eyes shone in the dimly lit barn. He never admitted it, but Zach knew all the same. He was about to enter a dark world where the line between friends and enemies was often blurred and always shifting. It was an atmosphere very much like prison. No doubt, the time he'd spent at Florence would serve him well.

Chapter 30

Dale

They ate dinner in silence. When they were done, Ann brought Walter up some soup. He seemed to be improving physically, although neither of Nicole's parents had recovered from the recent series of events which had taken their daughter's life.

Dale couldn't help but marvel at how Shane and Nicole's treachery had damaged morale in the house. Zach wasn't pulling his full weight and was setting a bad example for Colton and Dannyboy, who seemed to follow him around the way Duke followed Dale. The thought of his dog made Dale reach down and stroke the animal's fur. But their small enclave wasn't the only thing torn in two. The town was also divided on how to deal with the cartel and the direction Encendido should take if and when they ever managed to expel the drug-dealing thugs from their borders. *United we stand, divided we fall.* That old saying seemed truer now than ever.

But not all hope was lost. If Shane managed to end his long streak of failures in life and actually succeed at taking out Edwardo Ortega, then their chances of throwing off the yoke of bondage and oppression were that much greater. Sandy had told him about her meeting with Keith, how he was working for the resistance now—needless to say, news which Dale received with a healthy dose of skepticism—and that the competing resistance movements in town needed to come together before La Brigada showed up to squash any hopes of a successful rebellion.

Almost on cue, Zach cleared his throat and stood. "I wanted to let you know that I'll be leaving tonight," he said, rubbing his hands together against a chill that wasn't there.

"This late?" Brooke asked. "When will you be back?" She seemed to think Zach was stepping out to run an errand.

Dale could tell from his brother-in-law's voice that something else was going on.

"Maybe never."

"I don't understand," Brooke said. "Where are you going?" She turned to Colton, whose eyes were glued to the salt shaker on the table, a guilty flush coloring his cheeks. "Not you too. If this is a joke, I don't like it one bit."

A sad expression clouded Sandy's face. "Wherever you're going, it sounds like you already made up your mind."

Zach glanced over at Dannyboy and Colton. "You boys have anything you wanna say for yourselves?"

Colton stood, his eyes still downcast. "Yeah, Dannyboy and I will also be leaving."

Tears started to form in Brooke's eyes. Ann came down the stairs and said she could sense from upstairs that something was going on.

"This have anything to do with our differences of opinion?" Dale asked, scraping his empty plate with the tip of his dinner knife.

"Well," Zach said, "the truth is, we're joining the resistance."

Dale lifted his head. "That right?"

"Not just joining," Dannyboy added with pride. "Calvin Pike went and got himself killed and Zach's taking over."

Dale's heart sank. Losing Zach would be a blow to keeping the house well defended, no doubt. But suddenly Dale's hopes that the two groups might put aside their differences and come together seemed to be slipping away. "How convenient for you," was all Dale could say.

Zach let out a short burst of laughter. "Whacking the competition sounds like something I'd do, no doubt about it. But for once my hands are clean. The organization had a vacancy and apparently I was voted in unanimously. I guess your reputation isn't the only one that gets around."

"Then I don't need to tell you how important it is that you reach out to Nobel and coordinate your efforts."

The look on Zach's face shifted. Gone was the timid relative delivering a bit of sad news. The arrogant, stubborn side was back and in full force. "There's a lot that needs to be done. If Vickie wants to meet, she knows where to find me. I think you and everyone else here should join us. We could use the house as a forward operating base to launch attacks and question prisoners."

Zach's eyes were glowing, like a child dreaming about a shiny new toy. In this instance he would be playing soldier, except the pieces would be made of flesh and blood instead of plastic.

"I think you know where I stand on that," Dale said.

Zach scoffed, a gravelly sound which emanated from the back of his throat. "Yeah, I figured as much. The offer will stand in case you change your mind, although knowing you, it may be hard for you to take orders instead of doling them out. But I can assure you, I'll be a top-notch leader."

Dale went back to his plate. "I'm sure you will." His eyes rose to meet the other two. "When do you all leave?"

"Right away," Colton said, looking at his dad. "Apparently they're expecting us."

"I'll be taking the tank, of course, as well as the chopper I stored in your garage." Zach surveyed the calluses on his hands. "I can say it'll be nice not to be busting my hump doing manual labor anymore."

A few minutes of awkward conversation followed, after which Zach and the others gathered their things and said their goodbyes. Dale and the others stood by the driveway, the cool night air creeping up the sleeves of Dale's shirt and into his bones. He knew where he needed to go tomorrow morning and who he needed to speak with. Dale felt his mind racing in circles with concerns and possible outcomes, none of which looked good.

Chapter 31

The following morning, Dale and Brooke drove to Encendido Community College, west of town. After they pulled off Winrow Avenue and into the parking lot, their truck was approached by two men with AK-74s. It seemed Vickie's perimeter security had everything but a gate and a vehicle barrier arm.

"What's your business here?" one of them asked with a fair amount of hostility and aggression.

"I need to speak with Nobel," Dale answered rapidly. He was in a hurry and didn't have time for chitchat.

The guard looked past him to Brooke.

"She's my daughter."

The guard got on a walkie-talkie. "Inform Nobel that Dale is here to see her. Go ahead, sir," he said, waving them forward.

Dale rolled ahead, glancing in his rear view only to find that the two security men had melted from view.

Anyone patrolling the area who didn't belong would think the college was abandoned, an illusion Nobel apparently went to great lengths to maintain.

They parked the pickup and entered the main building through a set of large double doors into a long, wide hallway. Discarded papers and bits of trash littered the floor. In a corner lay a bulging knapsack, filled, perhaps, with textbooks and other school supplies. It was as if a stampede of students had rushed from the college for safety, the virus chasing them out the doors and through the streets. And in a way that was exactly what had happened. Except it had followed them all the way home, devastating families, neighborhoods and the country at large. Even Dale didn't know how far the desolation had spread.

A set of stairs to their right led down to the lower levels. On the top riser was the image of a circle, the letter V inside. "This way," he told Brooke who followed him closely, breathing hard. His daughter was scared and Dale couldn't exactly blame her.

Down two levels, they found a young man with dirty blond hair awaiting them.

"Caleb," Brooke shouted with relief.

He smiled and led them through a hallway and into a room buzzing with activity. On one wall was a large map of the county. Another showed Encendido. Specific landmarks and buildings were marked—the high school, the sheriff's office, the Teletech plant and plenty of others.

Men and women wearing black caps and matching shirts sped by them in every direction. These weren't the sleepy, unmotivated resistance fighters Dale had expected to find. They seemed organized and motivated and maybe in the middle of preparing for the big operation Keith had told them about.

Vickie was nearby, speaking with Betty Wilcox, when she spotted them and came over.

"You must have heard by now," she said, cutting right to the chase.

162

"About Zach?" Dale answered, jumping to the obvious conclusion.

"No, there have been more executions," Vickie told him, the anger ringing loudly in her voice.

"Again?" Brooke said.

"They won't stop until we get rid of these monsters." Vickie made that clear.

"What was their crime?" Dale asked. "Failing to pay an oxygen tax?"

Vickie grinned. "Trading with the enemy," she said.

Her words sliced into his flesh like a hundred tiny daggers. "Trading?"

"Pamela Steiger, David Halper and a handful of others."

Dale's heart froze in his chest. "Oh, no. What about Billy Forest?"

Vickie flipped through pages on a clipboard. "He's not on the list."

Relief flooded Dale's soul, but even so, that feeling of guilt wasn't going away.

"It's not your fault," she said, somehow knowing that he had been the enemy they'd been caught trading with.

"Aren't we going to move in to free them?" Dale sounded desperate.

She glared at him. "And risk the operation we're planning? If we moved in to save every person the cartel did harm to, we'd run out of people and fast."

"Those were our neighbors," Brooke said, grimacing.

Dale got Caleb's attention. "Why don't you show Brooke around?"

"Sure thing," Caleb said, taking Brooke by the elbow and easing her away.

When both of them were gone, Vickie asked him about Zach.

163

Dale filled her in on the events from the night before.

A look of gloom clouded her otherwise attractive features. "Do you expect your brother-in-law to be any more reasonable than Calvin?"

Shaking his head, Dale said: "Unfortunately, he's one of the most impulsive, pig-headed people I know."

Vickie scrunched her lips. "I've never understood how some men can be so blind to the bigger picture. They'd rather hand the entire county to Edwardo and his goons than work with a woman."

"Like the old saying goes," Dale said, "some people will cut off their nose to spite their face." He looked at her more closely, noticing a small mole on her right cheek. "Do you really think that's what it is, blindness?"

"Some days that's how it feels, especially with men like Calvin and Sheriff Randy. They may have been on opposing sides, but they were largely cut from the same cloth."

"That brings up something I was meaning to run by you," Dale said.

She eyed him curiously.

"I wanna set up a meeting, just me and Randy."

Vickie's eyebrows both rose at once. "I don't see why you'd wanna do that."

"Isn't it obvious? The cartel came in and stole the town right from under his nose. He was once the number two man. Now with Hugh Reid pushing up desert shrubs, he's fallen way down on the pecking order."

She still wasn't buying it. "I understand all that, but I'm just not seeing the payoff."

"Randy's got an ego the size of Arizona," Dale told her. "Don't you think he's already started weighing his options going forward? If we offered him the right deal, he and all his deputies might desert and join us. With the

164

cartel acting more and more like ISIS every day, he can't help but be looking for a way out."

"And once the dust settles, guess who'll come out smelling like roses and looking like a hero?"

Dale had considered that too. "If we stick together, we can contain Randy and his ambitions, maybe even find a way to be done with him altogether. Besides, with the army nowhere in sight, what alternative do we have?"

"You're starting to sound like Edwardo," Vickie said, giving him a look.

Dale didn't like that, even if it was only a joke.

"Listen," she said, "I'll talk with Keith and see if he can work something without blowing his cover."

"No," Dale cut in. "He's got enough on his plate. I'll take care of it myself. But mainly because there's something else I need Keith to do." Dale glanced over Vickie's shoulder to find Brooke field-stripping an AR with her eyes closed. A young girl, showing off in front of a boy she liked. What a difference from the girls of his generation. "Any chance that stockpile of weapons you got contains a silenced pistol?"

"It might," Vickie answered, laying out the words slowly. One of her eyes was half shut, as though she were anticipating what was coming next.

He told her about Shane's unique position on the inside. That the cartel was keeping him around for the day they could use him against Dale. And that he'd offered to assassinate Edwardo. "Keith will need to smuggle it in to him as soon as possible."

The idea intrigued her. "You know, it might just work. But if I do this, then you've got to do something for me."

Dale nodded. Now it was his turn to be worried. "I'm listening."

"If Zach's as much of a hothead as you claim he is, he's going to get a lot of innocent people killed."

165

"Believe me," Dale told her, "it's something of a specialty of his."

"If he can't control himself, he'll only drive the townspeople right into the arms of the cartel. You need to convince him to come on board and join us."

"He's a glory hog," Dale countered. "It won't be easy."

"Anything worth doing never is," she replied. "I know you can do it."

She walked away then, leaving Dale to wonder if he shared her faith in him.

Chapter 32

Zach

Zach was awoken by a firm knock on his door.

"Zero eight hundred hours, sir," the voice on the other side said. "Time to get up."

They had showed up last night to cheers from the men and women of the resistance movement. At last he'd found the devoted followers he always wanted. In a way, throughout Zach's whole life he'd felt like a preacher in search of a flock. For a long time he'd been lost out in the wilderness, but at long last he was finally home.

The look of pride on Colton's face at seeing the respect and hope in people's eyes was not lost on him. Every son wanted to believe his father was a superhero and now Colton's own dream was also coming true. And no one asked whether Zach had a criminal history, whether he'd ever killed a man. In the old world, those things would have held him back. Now they were the things you put at the top of your résumé. Street cred, as the kids liked to call it.

The knock again.

167

"I'm coming, darn it," Zach barked.

His first order of business upon arriving last night had been to christen the organization with a name. It needed to be something that would inspire confidence in its followers and fear in its enemies.

A few ideas had occurred to him before the light popped bright before his mind's eye. Encendido Patriot Militia (EPM). And those fighting for the cause would be called rangers. Hard to justify fighting against a group that stood for the ideals of the founding fathers and sounded as tough as anything the military could produce. Not everyone was crazy about having a name. Some tried to argue that it reduced them to a soundbite in a news headline and might distort what the movement really stood for. Zach assured them they'd learn to love it.

With the windows painted over, it was difficult to tell what time of day it was. But there were benefits. He had his own room at last, which meant privacy and perhaps down the road even some companionship. The EPM was coed and as their new leader, Zach felt entitled—no, obligated—to ride the wave he was on all the way into shore and, if possible, beyond.

Dressed, Zach exited his room and entered the church's main basement hall, only to discover everyone already assembled in three neat rows.

Nice touch.

At the head was Travis, followed by three of his lieutenants.

"Would you like to say a few words, sir?" Travis asked.

"Yes," Zach replied. He paced back and forth, making eye contact with each of those assembled. "I'm looking around and I see folks from all walks of life. At one time some of you were waiters and waitresses,

168

factory workers, accountants, lawyers. Some of you may have even been in the military."

No one said a thing, but Zach could see in their faces that he had their attention. He wasn't one for speeches, normally hated talking in front of a group, and yet somehow this had been different. He'd spoken from his heart and the words had come tumbling out.

"Although we may have arrived here from different places, each of us shares a common goal—to free our town from tyranny and get back our way of life. Now go do your duty."

The ranks scattered, each individual heading to varying work stations. The room was divided up into several sections. Intelligence-gathering was at the far end. Along the opposite wall were the briefing and mission planning areas. Next to them was communications. The final area was where classes were held on weapons and tactics.

Travis sidled up next to him.

"Quite a slick operation you've got here," Zach observed. "Something tells me Calvin didn't have much to do with this side of things."

"Calvin sure looked the part," Travis admitted. "But he couldn't inspire his way out of a paper bag."

"Things are different now," Zach assured him. "The EPM is about to start hitting back and hard. I want you to make a list of targets. Symbolic, strategic, write them all down. By the time we're done, our ranks will be swelling with volunteers while the cartel won't be able to walk down the street without looking over their shoulder."

"Can't wait," Travis said, grinning.

"I also wanna ask you about Nobel's group."

"What about them?"

"Well, for starters, do you think they pose a threat?"

Travis seemed to consider the question. "We haven't had any trouble with them so far, if that's what you're asking. They're usually busy running their own covert operations. Cloak-and-dagger type stuff. But I have heard she's sitting on a large cache of weapons…" Travis stopped short.

"Did I hear 'weapons' and 'large cache' in the same sentence?"

"Her husband ran a gun store," Travis explained. "When things with the virus got ugly, she apparently packed it all up and hid it somewhere safe. There's a rumor it's at the old community college under heavy guard, but that's about as much as we know. Calvin tried to find out more, but never got anywhere."

"Does the cartel know anything about this?"

Travis regarded him strangely. "They might, although those guys aren't lacking weapons, I can tell you that with certainty."

"They may not need them," Zach said. "But if I was the cartel, I wouldn't want that much firepower in circulation. If it really is the cache I'm picturing, it could arm enough folks to topple the cartel once and for all." Zach tapped his finger against his pant leg. "Work on those targets and leave this cache business to me."

"Will do." Travis started to walk away and then stopped. "We made the right decision bringing you in. I can see that now."

Zach's face lit up. "You don't know the half of it."

He found Colton and Dannyboy nearby in an orientation meeting. It was being taught by a cute blonde with a ponytail, a 1911 strapped to her leg.

He gave the two of them a knowing look. Here they were on the cusp of something of monumental importance and both of them were being led around by their libido. Zach waved over Dannyboy, whose face dropped.

"Don't be like that," Zach said. "There'll be plenty of time to flirt later. Right now I have a special mission for you."

Dannyboy perked up.

"I need you to gather some volunteers to our cause."

"You mean, in town?"

"Town may be too dangerous. There's Tombstone and South Bisbee to the east, Whetstone to the north and a few places in between. You explain the danger the cartel poses, and that as soon as they get Encendido locked up tight, their town will be next. Don't be scared to lay on the fear tactics. I don't think it's an exaggeration either. Take the Harley along with some supplies. And don't forget a weapon or two to defend yourself in case you run into trouble." Zach was starting to sound like the boy's father and shut his mouth. "All right, now get."

Dannyboy hollered with glee as he ran off to get his things together.

A few moments later, Zach watched the young man load the chopper before starting the engine, a deep rumbling growl that always gave Zach shivers. He was envious that he couldn't be the one riding the empty highways, spreading the word. But Zach had responsibilities now. Folks who depended on him for their freedom, for their very lives.

He nodded as Dannyboy pulled on his helmet and saluted. There was a good chance he'd never see his friend again. But Dannyboy wasn't just a friend, was he? No, the kid had become something of a son. But strong as that bond might be, it would never eclipse the one Zach shared with Colton, his own flesh and blood. During those dark days when the virus was ravaging his body, Colton had been Zach's will to live. And it was the memory of his son which had propelled him the many miles it took to reach home. He'd seen the look of pride in the boy's eyes. Kids couldn't hide stuff like that. Now that Zach finally had the chance, he wanted to earn it.

Chapter 33

Dale

"How did it go?" Ann asked, after they'd returned from the meeting with Nobel. She was standing by the pumphouse, trying to wash the paint off the side wall.

Duke scampered out, wagging his tail and begging to have his head scratched.

"About as well as can be expected," Dale told her. Sandy arrived and greeted him with a kiss, a sight which didn't seem to faze either Ann or Brooke. Although it was glaringly obvious by the way Brooke stared off into the distance and sighed heavily every minute or so that she had something else on her mind, or better yet, someone else.

Sandy and Dale exchanged a knowing glance.

"There's still a lot to do and hardly enough time to do it in," he said, just as another pickup pulled into the driveway. Duke began barking immediately. Ann came up with a 9mm pistol. Seeing it, Dale smiled and pushed the barrel down. "Easy, Annie Oakley," he said. "They're friends."

The pickup navigated the concrete pylons and came to a stop by the pumphouse. The three figures inside stepped out and Dale watched his daughter's face turn pink.

Caleb and the other three members of Vickie's organization greeted them. They introduced themselves as Jed, Roy and Tyrell. They were at least five years older than Caleb. Jed wore frayed overalls while Roy and Tyrell wore camo shorts and green shirts. But each man carried a long gun, a pistol and a chest rig with additional magazines.

"They're here to help around the house," Dale said. "And provide additional security now that Zach and the others have gone." The wound from their unexpected departure was still raw and Dale couldn't help feeling as though they'd abandoned him right when he needed them most. At least Vickie had been generous enough to lend them four of her own.

"I feel safer already," Brooke said, trying hard not to smile.

"You four can sleep downstairs in the living room. Ann will help you get settled."

The four men removed sleeping bags, pillows and other gear from the bed of the truck and followed Ann inside.

Once they set their things in order, Dale would take Roy and Tyrell to the basement to help him finish the tunnel. With any luck, the project wouldn't take more than a couple more days. As for Caleb and Jeb, there was still plenty of work to do outside, adding more foot traps, completing the ditch and tending to the chickens and the vegetable garden out back.

An hour later, with Roy digging away in the basement and Tyrell hauling up the hard-packed earth and dumping it outside, Dale sat down before the shortwave radio and signaled the sheriff's office.

"Encendido Sheriff's Office," a man responded.

Dale didn't recognize the voice. "Get Sheriff Gaines," he said.

"I'm afraid the sheriff isn't available."

"Tell him it's Dale Hardy. Tell him we need to talk."

The other end grew quiet for several minutes. Dale was about to hang up when Randy came on.

"I must say, you're the last person I expected to hear from," Randy said.

"We need to meet," Dale said, cutting the small talk short. "Can I trust you won't try to pull something stupid?"

A pause. "Of course you can trust me."

"Is anyone else listening in?" Dale asked. The question was a trap. Of course they were, but he wanted to see how Randy would answer. If he said no, the lie would only prove the sheriff wasn't really interested in meeting him man to man.

"You know there are, Dale."

Now it was Dale's turn to stop and consider the full range of risks he was about to expose himself to. "We need to speak, but it can only be you and me. Anyone else shows up and the meeting's off."

"What's this about?" Randy asked, sounding intrigued, but not trying to let on.

"Can't discuss it like this. I'm sure you understand."

"How do I know I can trust you? You did try to kill me, Dale. Don't think I forgot about that."

"I did," Dale admitted. "And sometimes I wish that shot hadn't gone wide. But there are some things that are bigger than an old feud between two stubborn bastards. You have my word. Now, will you agree to meet?"

There was another silence and this one seemed to last a while. "Where?"

"I'll have someone radio you in thirty minutes with the location."

"You're worried I'm going to get there first and set up an ambush," Randy said, sounding entertained that Dale could practically see inside his head.

"I wouldn't put it past you. There's trust and then there's trust. Let's stop playing games. If I see that you're alone, then we'll have words. I spot anyone else and I'll be gone before you know it."

"Fair enough," was Randy's final reply before the conversation ended for good.

Dale went upstairs and told a rather worried Sandy to wait thirty minutes and then radio the sheriff's office telling them where he would be.

Chapter 34

Apparently Sandy wasn't the only one who thought Dale shouldn't be going alone. When he got to his truck, he found Duke waiting there, wagging his tail.

"Not this time, boy," he told the dog. "But I'll return soon and we'll work on some drills out back."

Panting, Duke barked and continued to eye the truck. After a minute of angling, Dale was able to open the door a crack and slide past Duke into the driver's seat. "You watch the others while I'm gone," he said.

Dale rolled a few feet down the drive and stopped when he saw Caleb, Jeb and Brooke working on the trench. "I'll be back shortly," he said.

"All right," Brooke said, dismissively.

Dale couldn't help but chuckle as he pulled away.

The spot he picked was a landmark ten minutes west of town called the Devil's Pitchfork, a large saguaro cactus that looked a lot like Satan's favorite farming implement. The spot itself was on a rise, from which Dale would be able to keep an eye over the valley below, especially the main road that led out of Encendido. He waited in the truck, peering through a set of binoculars and sipping on a canteen of well water. Next to him were his three favorite weapons—one for long range, the second for medium and the last up close and personal. If Randy had any sense of self-preservation, Dale was confident he would do as he promised.

Several minutes passed before a lone dust cloud appeared along the road below. As the vehicle drew closer, Dale saw that it was a cruiser.

So far, so good.

Before long, it pulled up to where he was parked. Both men stayed in their vehicles, eyeing each other. At last, Dale opened his door and planted a foot on the hot dusty ground.

"I'll take it on faith that you're armed," Dale shouted.

Randy opened his own door. "Stupid not to be, especially out here where nearly everything out here will kill you soon as look at you."

"Sounds a lot like life in Encendido."

Randy grinned, the expression practically sealing his eyes shut.

"So how you wanna do this?" Dale inquired.

"Leave our weapons in our vehicles. Step out and spin around so we know nobody's cheating."

Dale thought it over. "Sounds fair."

They did so, both men stepping into the stifling desert air, making a full turn, one at a time, and standing there as though waiting for some third party to provide further instructions.

"You coulda picked a cooler place to meet," Randy complained. His cheeks and the edges of his ears were pink and wet with perspiration. "I'm just saying."

Both men walked toward each other, meeting somewhere in the middle. Fewer than five feet separated them, but this was about as close as either of them wanted to get.

"I'm here," Randy said. "And I don't have all day, so let's get to it."

"I wanna make you an offer," Dale said. "It's not one I'll make again, so I want you to think real hard before you answer."

Randy watched him, dark patches growing from his armpits. "I'm listening."

"You and I both know right now we aren't the problem."

The sheriff's eyes flicked to Dale's feet and then back. "The cartel," he said, knowing full well what his long-time adversary was getting at.

"Since they've arrived," Dale said, "things in town have gone from bad to worse."

"Yeah, well, if you hadn't been so hard-headed, we coulda found a more amicable solution."

"I didn't bring you all the way out here, Randy, in order to debate who was at fault. If you were doing what was in your heart, then more power to you. The truth of the matter is, the cartel's getting ready to chew what's left of this town up and spit it out. They already did the same to Hugh Reid and countless others."

"So what are you suggesting?" Randy said, that same arrogant smirk spread across his lips. "You wanna team up? Become best friends? Fight crime together?"

"I'm advocating a truce," Dale said flatly. "You give it whatever name you want. If we move on the cartel, I need your word your men won't interfere."

"And if I do? What's in it for me?"

"Your life," Dale replied. "Perhaps even a future in Encendido. You've done some horrible things, Randy. And I'm not only talking about what you tried to do to me and countless other residents in town. I'm talking about the biggest no-no. Number six on God's instruction manual. Good people were killed in cold blood and we have proof you were involved."

"Betty," Randy hissed.

"She's safe," Dale said. "But she's also a practical woman, Randy. You play your part and we can make the charges against you go away. One way or another, Encendido will be free of the cartel. When the chips fall, you'll need to make up your mind which side you wanna be on."

"While I consider your proposal, let me offer you a bit of advice. Your friends in the resistance movement need to stop blowing things up and taking shots at deputies and cartel members. It's only pushing Edwardo further over the edge. I'll tell you, if that crazy bastard had a nuke he'd have set it off by now, and right over the city center. The guy's that volatile. There's no telling how many he'll kill if he's pushed too far. It's not an exaggeration to say he'd order everyone butchered."

Randy was talking about Zach's new outfit and the havoc they'd wrought under Calvin's leadership.

"Tell him to ease off until you and your people are ready for the big push. If you can promise me that, I'll give you my word we won't interfere."

Randy put out his hand. Dale stared him in the eye, stepped forward and took it. They stayed like that for a full minute, squeezing hard enough to let the other man know they meant business, but just shy of breaking any bones.

Chapter 35
Zach

Peering through the binoculars, Zach watched two cartel members enter a bungalow across the road. Zach and his men were in an empty house on Laguna Street in the southeastern corner of Encendido. When he had asked Travis for targets they could hit, this had topped his list—a cartel outpost of sorts, designed to allow the criminal organization to project their dominance over this part of town.

The place had been under observation for two days when Zach had given the green light. From the intelligence they had managed to gather, anywhere from three to seven cartel members were stationed here at any one time. It seemed their main purpose was to patrol the neighborhoods, collecting taxes in the form of supplies, but mostly they were here to remind the locals who was in charge.

Zach glanced back at Travis on his left, Colton standing next to him. Eight other rangers were with them. Apart from .223 caliber assault rifles, each man carried a pistol and a tactical vest with plenty of extra ammo. Unlike the others, Colton carried a shotgun loaded with slugs designed to breach the front door if necessary.

The purpose of the operation was to bust in and send the cartel a very clear message.

"Everyone ready?" Zach asked, making a visual inspection of the men around him. Many of them gave the thumbs up. "Okay, let's do this."

The strike team moved toward the safehouse's front door, Zach in the lead. The last man stayed by the window to give one final look before they charged across the street and attacked the target.

"Go," came the okay from the window.

Zach pushed open the front door, ten men in full close-quarters battle gear behind him. This was the most vulnerable part of the operation. The adrenaline was pumping through Zach's veins as they reached the parched front lawn of the bungalow, and then the main entrance. He tried the handle and found it locked.

"Breacher," Zach called out to Colton, who ran up and fired the shotgun slug between the handle and the doorframe. Zach then took a step back and kicked it in, shouting as he entered the house. The place was littered with empty chip bags and beer cans. One cartel member sprang from the couch, reaching for the rifle at his feet. Zach and the two men covering him opened fire at once, riddling the man's body. He was dead before they stopped shooting. They then swept the rest of the house, one team moving left through the living room and another heading right down a hallway past the kitchen.

In the distance, Zach listened as they called, "Clear!" as each room was checked. He kicked open a bedroom door at the end of the hallway. A stained king-sized mattress lay on the floor, surrounded by more trash. They moved in. Colton, who was on Zach's right, covered his angle and shouted in alarm. A cartel member was halfway out the window. Colton opened fire with his shotgun, hitting the man under the armpit, opening up his chest. The thug collapsed, dead.

"Clear," a ranger called on Zach's left.

Seconds later, the team led by Travis found them and announced the rest of the house was clean.

"Find anything useful?" Zach asked.

"A few weapons and boxes of ammo. Also a bunch of handwritten orders. Seems half the time the cartel doesn't bother with shortwaves or walkie-talkies."

Perhaps they were worried about being monitored or having their messages recorded.

"Pack all that stuff up and begin setting the charges." Zach turned to his son, who looked pale. "This can't be your first blood?" he asked, puzzled by his son's reaction.

Colton shook his head. "No."

"Don't worry. It keeps getting easier. Believe me."

•••

They planted the charges in three rooms, connecting them to one another by wires. A piece of fishing line led from the front door handle to the detonator switch. As soon as the next cartel member pushed their way inside, the place would go sky high. Travis had originally advised using a single charge, but Zach's philosophy of 'go big or go home' had won out.

With that done, the strike team moved the bodies into the basement and retreated back to the house across the street. Zach felt it was important to know precisely how many cartel members the blast would eliminate. If they were lucky, an entire quick reaction force would show up to join the party. Once the blast rocked the house, Zach's team would finish off any remaining survivors before heading back to base.

The seconds and minutes ticked by at a glacial pace and Zach was beginning to wonder whether anyone would ever show up. Then a signal came from the lookout that a pair of dark SUVs were approaching. As they drew closer, Zach's heart began to gallop in his chest. After what they'd done to his biker crew, killing two cartel members felt good—killing another five or six, well, there were just no words.

The SUVs pulled into the driveway. One cartel henchmen exited the lead vehicle and headed for the house.

"Wait for everyone else," Zach shouted as the first guy reached the front door and stopped, his hand resting on the smooth wooden surface. He was calling back to the others, telling them to come. "That's right, the more the merrier. Why not have a party?"

Two more cartel members emerged and they opened the back doors. Maybe they were transporting VIPs. Zach could see this was going to be a bigger victory than he expected.

"Wait a sec," Travis said. "Who is that with them?"

The two cartel men opened the hatches on both SUVs and pulled out more people. Altogether they had ten women, their hands zip-tied and lashed together two by two. These weren't cartel women, they were Americans, townspeople from Encendido, probably picked up in some sort of raid. The lead guy was waving them all forward. He hadn't seen the hole in the door. Didn't realize yet that anything was amiss.

"We gotta stop them," Zach shouted, jumping to his feet and charging for the front door, the barrel of his rifle already on target. The two cartel men in the back turned and leveled their own weapons right as the house exploded, engulfing those standing nearby in a ball of deadly fire and flying debris.

The shockwave struck Zach in the chest, throwing him back into the front hallway of the house. Hands grabbed at him, lifted him up. It was Colton, petrified that his father had been killed.

The house across the street was engulfed in flames. On the front lawn were the remains of what had once been human beings.

Travis tried to call the operation a success, but Zach knew otherwise. They'd killed five cartel members and ten innocent women. Casualties of war, Zach kept telling himself over and over.

"Dad," Colton said, himself shocked at the sight, "are you okay?"

Zach stayed quiet. At the moment, he didn't have it in him to lie.

Chapter 36

Dale

Dale got to within a hundred yards of the old Baptist church before a handful of Zach's men intercepted him, peppering him with the usual questions before they let him through. Zach wasn't expecting him, but after hearing news of what had happened, Dale had rushed over as quickly as he could. Even pulling into the parking lot, he noticed a loose perimeter of snipers and riflemen, keeping watch. Dale parked the truck and headed for the entrance, where he was disarmed and asked the same batch of questions he'd answered moments before. Blood boiling, Dale couldn't help feeling as though he were on a 1-800 helpline.

To speak with Zach, please press one.

One.

You now have seven options.

Darn it.

"Let him through," Zach's voice said from the shadowed interior.

Dale entered, his eyes struggling to adjust to the dramatic change in lighting.

186

"You can never be too safe," Zach said, handing Dale back his pistol.

Dale looked around at the figures moving back and forth around them. "Can we speak somewhere private?"

"Follow me."

They entered what looked like an office. It had a wooden desk, papers and maps strewn across it, behind that a banker's lamp on a side table.

"Does it work?" Dale asked, pointing to the lamp.

Zach shook his head. "I'm looking at trying to get some juice hooked up. Realistically, though, it's looking more like I'll need to move the entire operation. Find a vacant farmhouse with some fertile land and maybe even a well. Of course it'll need to be fortified and powered by wind and solar."

Dale looked sympathetic. "I have some experience in that area if you need any help."

"I may just take you up on that." An awkward silence descended over the tiny room. Zach went and sat behind the desk. Dale took a seat opposite him. "If you came here to gloat, or if you came to say you told me so, I'm not interested."

"I came for neither," Dale told him honestly. "First off, let me say I'm sorry about what happened. I know your goal is to rid Encendido of the cartel and I respect that."

"Not just the cartel," Zach shot back. "Have you forgotten the many times Randy tried to have you killed? That he poisoned your brother against you and would love nothing more than to see you and everyone you love rotting in a shallow grave?"

"How can anyone forget that?"

Zach leaned forward, planting his elbows on the desk. "Guess I got confused, 'cause I didn't hear you mention the need to have Sheriff Gaines removed or tried for what he's done."

187

"Gaines will get what's coming to him in due time, Zach. Right now we're facing bigger problems, wouldn't you agree? La Brigada could show up at any time."

"You're not telling me anything I don't already know."

"Then you know you can't do this on your own," Dale said. "You need allies and everything that entails."

"You know, we were averaging ten new recruits every day," Zach countered.

"And after killing those ten women?"

The muscles in Zach's jaw clenched. "Fewer, but it'll pick up again, mark my words."

"That's not what I'm hearing."

"Enlighten me," Zach said, the doubt seeping out of every pore.

"First your organization blew up much-needed water trucks. Then, when you took the fight to the enemy for real, it resulted in the deaths of innocent townspeople. Sure, some cartel died, but even you can agree that driving our friends into the arms of our enemy is counterproductive."

"We've got other attacks in the works," Zach said defiantly.

"I may be the last person you're willing to listen to," Dale continued. "But I respectfully ask that you cease and desist. As we speak, we're in the middle of two major operations. One of them would effectively cut Ortega's fighting force in half." It was the tentative truce Dale had secured with Randy. But based on Zach's earlier reaction, there was no way he was going to fill him in on that. "The other involves an attempt on Edwardo's life."

Zach sat up straight. "How do you plan on getting that close? You're not that good of a shot."

"Not me," Dale said. "Someone else has the job."

188

Leaning back in his chair, Zach laced his fingers behind his head and stared at the ceiling as he rocked in contemplation. Suddenly the chair became still. "Don't tell me you got Shane to do it."

"I can't talk about details," Dale told him.

Zach burst out laughing. "For your sake I hope you didn't. That sap couldn't hit a fish in a barrel."

The steady rhythm of Dale's heart kicked up a notch. Zach wasn't calling Shane a bad shot. Shane's work at the range proved otherwise, but Zach was saying Dale's brother was a natural-born loser—words Dale had thought about often, even if it hurt to hear those words coming out of someone else's mouth.

"Now's the time we come together," Dale said, cutting through Zach's pessimism. Seemed Dale's real challenge was how to convince a guy like Zach not to shoot himself in the foot. It was a difficult proposition and Dale could feel the chance for reconciliation being swept away in a violent sandstorm.

"Word around here," Zach said, twirling his thumbs, "is that Vickie's sitting on a cache of weapons. Most of my guys brought what they had. We got a few nice weapons systems, but most of it's fairly old. Modern, reliable firepower, that's where the cartel's really got us beat."

Dale saw exactly where his brother-in-law was headed. "Will a few weapons help to bridge the gap, Zach? Is that what you're saying?"

"Can't hurt."

A knock came at the door.

"Come in," Zach said, still leaning back.

Travis entered. "We've just received word that Edwardo Ortega's been killed in an assassination."

Both men grew rigid, then looked at one another.

"Any word on the assassin yet?" Dale asked, tension forcing the fingers of his right hand into a fist.

189

"He was killed at the scene, apparently," Travis said, coolly. "Was he one of yours?"

Dale nodded and tried to say yes, but no words came out.

Chapter 37

Zach

After news of Ortega's death, Zach was quick to usher Dale out of his headquarters. Now that the cartel's leader had fallen, he realized this was the time to act. A strong enough assault by the EPM would surely send what was left of the cartel fleeing back across the border in disarray. Dale could play the diplomat and 007 all he liked, but what really mattered was hot lead cutting through cartel bodies.

Zach found Travis and two of his sublieutenants standing over a table in the operations area. A handmade drawing of the town showed the two major bases used by the cartel—the Teletech plant and Mayor Reid's mansion.

"We should assault the sheriff's office as well," Travis said, about to circle it.

"Not yet," Zach countered. "Sheriff Gaines and his deputies will be dealt with once we cut out the biggest cancer. Do we have enough men to strike both the plant and the mansion at once?"

"We've got a total of eighteen rangers," Travis told him. "But deploying them all means only a handful of support personnel will remain to defend the church."

Zach could feel his fingers itch the way they did whenever he hit the craps tables in Vegas. "We'll commit them in equal number against both objectives. And arm whoever's staying behind to keep watch while we're gone."

What they lacked in sophisticated weaponry, they made up for in transportation. Zach had already decided the Brinks truck would lead the assault on the mansion, the spot they expected the largest concentration of Ortega's men. Added to that were an assortment of SUVs and pickup trucks they kept concealed around the neighborhood, all part of creating the illusion that the church was empty.

It took another hour to finish gathering the vehicles and prepping the weapons and ammo. There wasn't much in the way of body armor, which meant the assault would need to be lightning fast in order to prevent a prolonged battle. Zach was hopeful that by splitting his forces into two nine-man teams and striking both targets at once, he could deliver a knockout blow. Faced with such a dramatic reversal, he was confident Randy, the king of self-preservation, would see the writing on the wall and stand down.

Those ten women at the safehouse will not have died in vain. It was a mantra Zach kept repeating as the time for departure drew nearer.

•••

Dale

Dale and Sandy were meeting with Nobel at her headquarters. There was more activity than usual. The place seemed to be on high alert.

"I know you must have mixed feelings," Nobel said reassuringly. "But your brother's death will not be in vain."

"The whole thing still doesn't feel real," he told them.

Sandy rubbed his back. "The two of you had issues, but what family doesn't? All he wanted was for you to be proud of him."

Dale *was* proud of his brother. Although the deep pain from his treachery was still there, he also knew that Shane's commitment to make amends had counted for something.

"How did your meeting with Zach go?"

Shaking his head, Dale said, "Not as well as I'd hoped. Doesn't look like he's going to budge."

"Even after that botched operation?" Sandy asked, incredulous.

"I don't think he saw it that way," Dale replied. "They took out a few cartel members and sent them a clear message. Anyone else who got hurt was purely collateral damage. But our meeting ended when news came through that Ortega had been killed."

"News has been spreading all over town," Sandy said. "Is there a chance the cartel could simply pack up and leave town?"

"There might have been," Nobel said. "But not anymore."

"What do you mean?" Dale asked.

"Not long after Ortega's assassination, our forward observers reported seeing a long line of cartel vehicles entering Encendido from the south. We believe Edwardo's father, the drug lord Fernando Ortega, was at the spearhead of La Brigada de Los Asesinos."

Sandy's hand covered her mouth.

"What does that mean for our chances of forcing them out of town?" Dale asked.

"It means we'll need every man and woman we can get," Nobel told him, a somber look on her face. "If we remain splintered, they'll likely destroy us piecemeal. That was why your mission to win over Zach was so vital."

"He mentioned the cache of weapons you're sitting on. Said he'd be open to some form of cooperation if you shared what you had."

Nobel shook her head. "The legend of my weapons cache has grown in the telling many times over. I do have long guns and pistols, but I'm usually credited with being able to outfit a battalion and that is simply not true."

Dale looked disappointed. "I'm afraid that was our only bargaining chip."

One of Nobel's lieutenants came and whispered in her ear. The change on her face was immediate and worrisome.

"More bad news?" Dale asked.

"Unfortunately, yes. I just received a report that Zach is on the offensive."

The blood drained from Dale's face. "Does that yahoo know the cartel's been reinforced, maybe even with La Brigada?"

"Impossible to say," Nobel replied. "An attack against those odds will be suicide."

"Then maybe we need to move in ourselves," Dale shot back.

"It'll be chaos," she said. "None of our forces will be coordinated. They're just as likely to start firing on one another as they are the enemy."

"At the very least I need to warn him."

194

Nobel didn't seem to like that idea either. "There's nothing you can do. Getting yourself killed won't help either."

"I'm not only thinking about Zach. If I can intercept and convince them to retreat, then maybe we can regroup and launch the assault together."

"There's more to it than that," Nobel said. "I can see it in your eyes. This is personal."

"My nephew's probably with them," Dale admitted. "I can't sit back and watch him being led to his death. Can you spare a few agents?"

Nobel dropped her eyes, likely wondering how to say no without losing Dale's support completely. "I can give you two."

"Thank you," he said, reaching out to her. "Any word on where they were headed?"

"The report was sketchy," she replied. "But a Brinks truck looked like it was speeding toward Hugh Reid's old mansion."

Chapter 38
Zach

They were about a minute away from what was once Mayor Reid's house and now served as a barracks for the cartel's enforcers. Zach was behind the wheel of the Brinks truck, charging north along El Camino Real. Colton was riding shotgun, his index finger tapping nervously against the stock of the shotgun resting between his legs. In the back were three other rangers, fully loaded with gear and weapons. The other four men who were part of Zach's unit trailed behind them in two pickup trucks.

Already the Brinks truck had come in handy, crashing through a cartel checkpoint on the corner of El Camino Real and Cardinal. Zach would have given anything to have a picture of their faces as they saw the giant armored truck barreling down on them. He scooped the walkie up off the dashboard and depressed the actuator with his thumb.

"Travis, this is Zach. We're nearly at our objective. Report."

His radio crackled with static. "Almost at the Teletech plant," Travis said. "Little to no resistance so far."

Zach smiled. "Sounds like we caught 'em with their pants down. Sweep through and don't bother leaving any survivors. See you back at base."

"Roger that," Travis confirmed.

The truck roared down Hugh's street and Zach pointed at a large gated house on the corner. "There it is." The mansion itself was far back from the road, positioned at the end of a long semicircular driveway. Many of the windows on the second story looked like they'd been reinforced. There was a chance they might come under heavy fire, which was why it was important to get as close as possible.

"The front gate's closed," Colton said, holding onto his shotgun with one hand and the door grip with the other.

"Not for long," Zach replied, pushing down on the accelerator seconds before the Brinks truck crashed through the gate, flinging both metal doors off their hinges and into the air. Almost at once, rounds pinged off the hood and roof of the truck. Which was precisely what Zach wanted. Better that he took the fire than the more vulnerable trucks following them. He swung around the circular driveway and pulled up the truck right next to the front door. Two cartel members came out of the house as one of the men in the back, a ranger named Peter, pushed the barrel of his AR out the side gun port and opened up, cutting the men to pieces.

"Stay close," Zach told Colton, as he grabbed his own AR. A second later everyone was out of their vehicles and heading toward the entrance. Zach took the lead, moving inside, scanning right and left for threats. Colton and the others were right behind him, making sure to cover every possible angle.

197

"Peter," Zach said. "Take five men and sweep the lower levels. The rest, stay on me. We're going upstairs."

Instead of one, there were two curved staircases which rose to a common landing some twenty feet up. They climbed them at a good clip, being careful not to move too fast. A balcony wrapped around the staircase, which those in the rear covered to avoid getting shot in the back as they ascended. Once the house was eventually safe, they would link up with Travis' group at the Teletech plant and help clear that out as well.

At the top of the staircase they came to a long hallway. "Colton, you and I will go right. Alex, you and Josh go left." They nodded and moved off.

Zach padded down the hallway, making sure to take the lead. Several rooms were on either side of them. He cursed Reid and his opulence. Checking each of these would take time and expose them to even more danger. Father and son worked their way through a handful of rooms, their luck holding firm.

By the fourth, something akin to muscle memory began to set in. Zach would push open the door and enter scanning left while Colton would move to the right. Then each of them would check closets, bathrooms and under the bed before moving onto the next. The Brinks truck had taken fire from the second floor, so Zach was quite sure there were at least a few cartel members present. He had to stay sharp, no matter how many times they were forced to repeat the same clearing technique.

They were onto the fifth room when they took fire.

As usual, Zach pushed his way inside, moving left, Colton right. A cartel member popped up from behind the bed with an AK and got two rounds off before Colton blew him back against the wall with a chestful of double-aught buck.

198

Zach's eyes were saucer-shaped and his heart slamming against his chest. He looked at Colton for wounds, then himself, and found none. Two large holes had been punched into the gyprock above the door frame.

"Good shot, son," Zach said, patting the boy on the shoulder.

Colton smiled. "I guess I'm not just another pretty face."

"Far from it," Zach said, winking.

At the end of the corridor was a room with an open door. If Zach's sense of direction was as good as he hoped it was, the windows in that room should look out over the driveway. Moving with a purpose, he and Colton came to a bend in the hallway which curved to the left. They would clear the room with the open door first, then move on.

Zach drew in a deep breath and stepped inside. The immediate view which greeted them was a pair of open windows, sandbags and odd bits of furniture stacked around them. An improvised firing position. But no signs of life. As usual, Zach moved left, Colton right.

There was a large, gilded bathroom, glittering before him. Zach would start by clearing that. He'd only taken two steps in that direction when the shots rang out, three of them in quick succession from an assault rifle. He spun to see Colton fall to the ground, and the barrel of a long gun sticking out from behind the open door. Zach shouted as he leveled his AR and filled the door with holes, shredding the cartel enforcer hiding behind it. The man fell forward, only his head and torso visible, and Zach kept on shooting. His rifle clicked empty but still he continued to pull the trigger.

That must have been the sound the grunt in the closet was waiting for because he charged out with a 9mm pistol. Zach threw his AR at the man, smacking him in the face with the rifle butt. The cartel enforcer recoiled for a moment, giving Zach the time he needed to pull his own pistol and start firing. Two shots struck the attacker's chest, the other two his head. He tumbled back into the closet dead.

Then came sounds of men charging down the hallway. Zach pivoted in that direction and leveled his pistol.

"Whoa, it's us," Alex shouted. Josh was next to him. Both men's eyes scanned the scene, settling on Colton, who was lying face down. Still in shock, Zach dropped to his knees and turned his son over. There were three large exit holes in his chest and a trail of blood running from the side of his mouth. He wasn't breathing. Zach put the pads of his blood-soaked fingers to his neck and didn't find a pulse. He pulled his son in close and wept.

Just then Zach's walkie came to life. "We need backup," Travis shouted. "Zach, are you there?"

Zach was rocking back and forth, still holding Colton. Alex reached over and grabbed his walkie. "Travis, this is Alex. What's going on?"

Travis sounded out of breath. "This place is crawling with cartel. It's like we hit a hornets' nest. We engaged the guards out front and men just came swarming from every direction. Fernando Ortega's here and he's brought plenty of reinforcements. There must be fifty of them, maybe even a hundred. We're pinned down. If you don't get here quick, we're all dead."

Then came the sound of a truck roaring into the driveway. "What now?" Josh said, heading to the window. A second later, he turned to the others. "It's Dale."

Chapter 39
Dale

Dale, Sandy and both of Nobel's agents rushed into Reid's mansion, not entirely sure what to expect. Five of Zach's rangers came around the corner and confronted them before realizing they were friendlies.

"Where's Zach?" Dale demanded.

Peter pointed up the stairs. "He took a group to clear the second floor. We were just about to head up there to check on them."

"Where are the other rangers who are part of your offensive?"

"They're at the Teletech plant," he replied, sounding unsure if he should have said anything.

"Fernando's in Encendido and he's brought La Brigada with him," Sandy told them.

"If they aren't here," Dale added, "it means they're at the plant. Your men might be walking into a trap."

"Are you sure about that?" Peter asked, starting up the stairs and then stopping.

Zach and the other rangers stood on the top riser, carrying a lifeless Colton by his arms and legs.

"Oh, no," Sandy said in horror.

Dale felt sadness and then anger bubbling up from the deepest parts of him. This was precisely what he'd feared most, that Zach's carelessness would destroy the only worthwhile thing he'd ever created—his son.

Dale rushed to check Colton's vitals.

"He's dead," Alex said. "I'm sorry."

Dale bit back the tears threatening to overwhelm him. Beside him, Sandy was crying. He put an arm around her.

"What did you do?" Dale shouted, shaking Zach.

"It wasn't his fault," Alex said, trying to intervene. "Colton was shot in the back by a cartel member hiding behind a door."

Dale's fiery gaze met Alex's. "Of course it was Zach's fault. That's his son. It was his job to keep him safe."

Zach's face remained expressionless.

"We don't have time for this," Alex told them. "Travis and the others are pinned down at the plant."

"Here, take my truck," Dale said, tossing Alex his keys. "All of you, meet us back at the community college." He looked at Sandy. "That includes you."

"You aren't heading to the plant alone," she said, and it was more of an order than it was a question.

"Of course not. Zach and I will take his armored truck, so he can save what's left of his men."

Zach regarded him with soulless eyes. It looked as though his son's death had also killed a part of his soul. There would be time for tears and self-recrimination later. Right now there were men who needed saving.

•••

Dale pulled the Brinks truck out of the driveway as Zach strapped himself into a seat at the back. Alex had given them the walkie, which Dale now handed to Zach.

"See if you can find out whether anyone's still alive," Dale ordered, tossing the walkie into his lap.

Zach glanced down at it as though it were a foreign object.

"You're gonna need to snap out of your funk, Zach, and real quick."

Tears were streaming down Zach's cheeks as he put the walkie to his lips. "Travis, you there?"

No response.

The plant wasn't more than a few minutes' drive and already Dale could hear the sound of gunfire growing louder.

Zach called out to them again, but all that came back was a garbled response, punctuated by the deafening roar of a gun battle.

Ahead was an SUV parked sideways, blocking the road. Three cartel enforcers were standing next to it, but not facing the oncoming Brinks truck. They were facing the Teletech plant down the street. This must be a cordon Fernando had created to ensure that none of the attackers managed to break out.

"Hold on," Dale said, accelerating.

The three cartel goons turned around about a second before Dale plowed into them. The Brinks truck shuddered violently as it blasted the SUV, sending it spinning off the road, scattering the dead bodies of the three men who had been standing before it.

As they drew closer, so too did the sound of gunfire.

"When I give you the signal, you need to pop that door open so they can climb onboard," Dale said.

Zach nodded in a rare display of subservience.

In depressions on either side of the road were two pickup trucks. The one on the left was on fire, two dead rangers lying next to it. On the right was Travis, one of his arms covered in blood, crouching behind the wheel well. Beside him was another ranger, who was firing back at the cartel members as they closed in. Dale pulled next to the pickups and hit the brakes. The truck skidded to a stop as incoming rounds began impacting the vehicle. Some pinged off the armored body while others struck the bullet-resistant glass, causing spider webs to form.

"Now," Dale called to Zach who swung open the door and charged out, braving the hail of bullets coming at them. The one ranger grabbed a wounded man and retreated to the vehicle, providing covering fire with his pistol as he did. Zach reached Travis, slung his lieutenant's good arm around his neck and carried him toward the open door.

"This windshield's about to give," Dale shouted. Already much of it had become milky white from incoming rounds, making it difficult to see.

"We have two more wounded," Travis said weakly. Zach charged out again, returning a minute later with another man.

Some cartel goons who had circled around their position popped up, firing into their exposed flank. Now rounds began to penetrate the weakened windshield. Dale ducked behind the dashboard for cover.

From the side door, two rangers returned fire on the cartel enforcers, wounding one and keeping the others' heads down while Zach scrambled back with the last survivor.

They slammed the door shut and shouted for Dale to drive. He put the truck in reverse and floored it. The engine roared as Dale used the side mirrors to make sure he stayed on the road. The front of the truck was still getting peppered with fire and Dale worried his heart might seize in his chest. When at last they reached the open street, Dale hit the brakes and turned the wheel hard to the right. The lumbering truck did a one-eighty, suddenly facing south. But the windshield was so badly damaged Dale was driving blind. His Mossberg had been on the seat next to him and was now on the floorboard. He scooped it up and used the butt to knock out what was left of the windshield. It would leave them exposed on the drive back to the college, but at least they'd be able to see.

By the time they reached Nobel's headquarters, one of the wounded rangers had died. Out of Travis' original nine-man team, only three remained. The situation wasn't looking good for the resistance. The EPM was diminished in number and largely demoralized. Meanwhile, Fernando Ortega had rolled into town right in the nick of time, saving the cartel's wobbling hold over Encendido. It was frightening how quickly the winds of fortune could turn against you. Those were the thoughts spiraling through Dale's mind as they sped into the college's parking lot. Outnumbered and probably outgunned, could the resistance movements finally come together or was it already too late?

Chapter 40

They arrived and quickly shuttled the wounded into a makeshift emergency room on the college's main floor. Betty was there, along with a handful of others who possessed basic medical knowledge.

Zach, Dale and Sandy stood over Colton's body as it was laid on a table in what had once been a classroom and was now a morgue. Nearby was the other dead ranger they'd attempted to rescue from the Teletech plant.

"We didn't get everyone out," Zach said, with a grimace. He was fighting to hold on.

Dale knew he was right. Travis' team had gone in with nine rangers, but only three had made it back alive. Maybe once this was all over they might find a safe opportunity to go back and offer the others a proper burial.

"I'd like him to be buried at the house," Dale said, studying Colton's eyes, futilely willing them to open.

Zach remained quiet for a moment before answering. "I think that's a good idea. I know he'd want to be next to his mother."

Dale nodded. He'd already considered that. "We can bring her too, when time permits."

Sandy put an arm around Zach, who stared at his son, his eyes roadmaps of sorrow and no doubt of guilt.

Travis came in a few minutes later, his left arm bandaged above the elbow. "Sir, I informed headquarters that we were here."

"That was fast," Sandy said, studying his arm.

He grinned. "Bullet missed the bone. I was lucky, I guess." Travis saw the change his comment evoked in Zach and bit his lip. "If there's anything I can do, boss, just let me know."

"There is," Zach replied, holding out his gun. "If you have any mercy in you, you'll take my pistol and put a bullet between my eyes."

Travis shook his head.

"Can we have a minute?" Dale asked the others.

"Of course," Sandy said, and she led Travis from the room.

When they were alone, Dale turned to Zach. "You left when your son was only a boy and returned to find a man standing in his place," Dale said, struggling against his own wave of emotions. "I loved him like a son too, Zach. And I wish I could take credit for the man he eventually became, but I can't."

Zach swallowed hard and his throat made a loud clicking noise. "Neither can I. That was his mother's doing," he said. "She deserves the credit. Even before I got sent away I was too busy chasing after a good time or the next big score to really realize what I was missing. They only take their first step once, learn to ride a bike once, graduate from high school once. I missed those moments, even though for some of them I was still around. I just couldn't be bothered, and that's what kills me the most. When I made it out of prison I swore to myself this time things would be different. That I'd be a

207

positive role model for him to follow. And all I managed to do was get him killed." Zach put the pistol to his temple.

"No, Zach, don't," Dale shouted. "That isn't the answer. It's not what Colton would've wanted. He worshiped you. I could see it in his eyes."

Tears streamed down Zach's cheeks. The veins in his neck bulged.

"When you showed up, it was as though Colton had finally found his purpose," Dale continued. "I won't lie. A part of me was jealous. Why didn't he look at me in the same way? But the answer was obvious. The special bond between father and son is something impossible to duplicate and often impossible to deny. I was always the responsible one and yet most of my old man's attention always seemed to be on Shane, the screw-up. For years, I resented him for that till finally I understood. He wasn't only doing it for my brother, he was doing it for himself. I guess deep down that's why we do anything. That same force brought you and Colton together and gave you a few precious weeks together. That's a second chance few fathers ever get."

The pistol in Zach's hand wavered, then began to descend, first past his nose, then his chin before settling back into his holster. As it did, a figure appeared in the doorway.

"I showed up at headquarters and they said you were here. Oh, am I interrupting something?"

Both men turned at once.

It was Dannyboy. "I got something you gotta see," he said before his eyes shifted to Colton's corpse on the table next to them and his smile melted into a frown.

The three men spoke for a few minutes before they left the room.

"What was it you wanted to show us?" Dale asked.

Dannyboy led them downstairs and into Nobel's command center. Assembled there were fifteen to twenty burly-looking bikers, clad in black leather vests and red bandanas, with an assortment of handlebar mustaches and long scraggly beards.

"They're a chapter of the Bandidos. Met them in a bar near Tucson and told them what the cartel had done," Dannyboy said, grinning. "Turns out the two groups have a long-standing feud and were anxious for some payback."

"So what do you say then?" Dale asked, eyeing Zach and the rings around his swollen eyes.

Zach glanced down at Dale's hand, contemplating the offer.

"I was pig-headed," he said. "I see that now as clear as day. It's just too bad I had to lose something so dear to me in order to figure that out." He shook Dale's hand. Those around them stopped what they were doing and applauded.

Nobel was there too. "United we stand," she began.

"And divided we fall," Zach replied.

There was more applause before Walter and Ann came forward. The old man was on crutches and being helped along by his wife. "Now that you two have kissed and made up," Walter said, bracing himself against the table, "it's time to get down to business." He unfurled a map of Encendido marked with key strategic positions. "I've had some time to think these last few days and I've come up with a plan."

One of Nobel's communications people appeared next to Dale and told him someone was on the shortwave asking for him, said it was urgent.

"Did they say who it was?" he asked.

"I believe her name was Brooke."

Dale's blood dropped five degrees.

He followed the man to the radio room and punched the mic's actuator switch. "Honey, is everything all right?"

"You need to come home right away," his daughter said. She didn't sound afraid at all. She sounded excited, elated even.

"What's going on?"

"Caleb's already out there talking to them. And I had to put the muzzle on Duke so he wouldn't hurt anyone."

"Slow down, Brooke," Dale told her. "I don't understand what you're saying."

"They're here, Dad. And I can hardly believe it."

"Who?" he asked, starting to lose his patience.

"The army. They've finally come."

Dale and the radio operator looked at one another. An involuntary smile began to spread across Dale's face. Fate *was* a funny thing. She could hide when you wanted her the most and appear just when you thought she'd gone away.

He turned to the comms operator. "Tell Nobel and the others the good news and that I'm headed home to fill the army in on the cartel's activities in town."

The comms man nodded as Dale ran from the room and headed for his truck.

Chapter 41

The drive home felt like an eternity. Dale had thought it safest to skirt around the outer edge of town in order to avoid any cartel forces fanning out to locate the resistance's base of operations. Coming in from the west, Dale saw three Humvees parked along the road, each armed with .50 caliber machine guns and manned by a gunner. He brought the truck into the driveway and parked a few yards from an officer and his men, all dressed in desert camo. Brooke was with them, along with Caleb, both beaming with smiles and excitement. Dale popped out of the truck, trying to temper his enthusiasm. The resistance had done a good job containing the cartel and he wanted to make sure they got their fair share of the credit.

"Mr. Hardy," the officer said in a Georgia accent, a tuft of silver hair poking out from beneath his helmet. "My name is Captain James Lee."

Dale wasn't sure whether to salute him, but opted instead to shake the man's hand.

"What took you guys so long?" Dale asked, half joking. "Our town's been taken over and we've been struggling to hold onto it."

"The whole country's been affected," Captain Lee said. The soldiers with him were admiring the pumphouse. "Your daughter here told us about how the cartel came in and killed the acting mayor."

"True, but things were already bad enough before all that happened," Dale explained. "The sheriff was expropriating people's land and resources. Ruling with an iron fist. They tried to do the same to me."

The captain looked around. "I can see they didn't get very far."

Dale laughed. "That's right. Listen, I'm not here to tell you gentlemen how to do your jobs, but the sooner the cartel's removed from Encendido, the quicker folks around here can get on with their lives."

"Are you armed, Mr. Hardy?" the captain asked.

"As I should be," Dale replied, motioning down to the pistol at his side.

"For our safety, sir, I'm going to ask that you remove the weapon for now. It's only a precaution."

Dale's features fell. "I'm not the enemy," Dale explained. "I already told you, as we speak a renowned drug lord's taken up residence in our town. If he isn't stopped he'll start gobbling up the other towns until Arizona and every other state along the border belongs to him."

"We're all on the same side," Captain Lee assured him.

"I'm sorry, Captain, but I can't comply. I'm no danger to you or your men, I can assure you."

"Subdue them," Captain Lee ordered.

Three soldiers lunged at Dale while a fourth kept his M4 Carbine pointed in his direction. A handful of other soldiers grabbed Caleb and Brooke and pushed them down, fastening their hands with zip ties.

"Are you people stupid?" Dale said as he was wrestled to the dusty ground. Once he was zipped and disarmed, the soldiers lifted him back onto his feet.

"Place them in one of the Humvees," Captain Lee ordered.

"This is insane," Dale shouted as he and the others were led away. "You're supposed to protect us, not imprison us."

They were shoved into the backseat of the lead Humvee. The temperature inside was scorching and it smelled like dirty socks.

Tears were forming in Brooke's eyes. "Why are they doing this?" she asked.

"I have no idea," Dale said, his eyes searching the vehicle's interior for clues to the unit's origin. "Did you notice anything odd before?" Dale asked them.

"What do you mean?" Caleb and Brooke both asked at once.

"Anything strange when they showed up, anything at all."

Brooke scrunched her nose. "Well, one of the men had a funny accent."

"Funny how?" Dale asked.

"I don't know, sounded weird, French or Eastern European. I'm not sure, maybe it's nothing."

Dale's eyes were scanning the dashboard when they froze on a pair of dog tags dangling from a hook. He tilted his head until he could make out what was written there and seeing it sucked the air out of his lungs.

On the dog tags were the words...

… La Brigada de Los Asesinos.

Thank you for reading Defiance Book 2!

I'm always grateful for a review. Any thoughts, comments or feedback can be sent to my email: williamhweberauthor@gmail.com

If you enjoyed Defiance, then you're sure to love Last Stand:
Last Stand: Surviving America's Collapse (Book 1)
Last Stand: Patriots (Book 2)
Last Stand: Warlords (Book 3)
Last Stand: Turning the Tide (Book 4)

Other books by William H. Weber
Long Road to Survival (Book 1)
Long Road to Survival (Book 2)

Made in the USA
Columbia, SC
14 February 2024